*"You've done it now, you know.*

"I can tell you that at least one person inside that house has noted the fact that we're holding hands."

So?" Ethan asked, not willing to let go. Her hand fit his perfectly. The simple act didn't feel awkward or forced but totally comfortable. He hoped this could be a sign of a possible change in the way she felt about him and, ultimately, about *them*.

"So they'll be talking about it. Wondering. Asking questions."

Ethan shrugged. "I don't mind if you don't." *Lord, am I moving too fast for Your will?* he prayed as they stepped inside of the Edwards household. *Am I doing the right thing?*

D0822827

**AISHA FORD** resides with her parents and younger sister in Missouri. Through her writing, Aisha hopes to present a message of complete trust in Jesus Christ. "The best guide for living is to follow the biblical example of Jesus—the route by which we will reap the most lasting rewards," Aisha says. "Though none of us is perfect, God is the inventor of grace—and He is patient above and beyond what we can ask or imagine." Visit Aisha's website at http://www.aishaford.com

## HEARTSONG PRESENTS

Books by Aisha Ford
HP362—Stacy's Wedding
HP405—The Wife Degree

Don't miss out on any of our super romances. Write to us at the following address for information on our newest releases and club membership.

Heartsong Presents Readers' Service
PO Box 721
Uhrichsville, OH 44683

FIC
FOR

10-02 donated

# Pride and Pumpernickel

*Aisha Ford*

631

BEULAH BAPTIST CHURCH
LIBRARY

*Heartsong Presents*

This book is dedicated to everyone who ever had a List.

**A note from the author:**
*I love to hear from my readers! You may correspond with me by writing:*

> **Aisha Ford**
> **Author Relations**
> **PO Box 719**
> **Uhrichsville, OH 44683**

**ISBN 1-58660-472-4**

**PRIDE AND PUMPERNICKEL**

© 2001 by Aisha Ford. All rights reserved. Except for use in any review, the reproduction or utilization of this work in whole or in part in any form by any electronic, mechanical, or other means, now known or hereafter invented, is forbidden without the permission of the publisher, Heartsong Presents, PO Box 719, Uhrichsville, Ohio 44683.

All Scripture quotations, unless otherwise indicated, are taken from the HOLY BIBLE, NEW INTERNATIONAL VERSION®. NIV®. Copyright © 1973, 1978, 1984 by International Bible Society. Used by permission of Zondervan Publishing House. All rights reserved.

All of the characters and events in this book are fictitious. Any resemblance to actual persons, living or dead, or to actual events is purely coincidental.

*Ccver design by Ron Hall.*

PRINTED IN THE U.S.A.

## one

Dana Edwards sat at a booth taking notes on the general state of things around her. The early Saturday morning breakfast rush slowly ebbed, and while employees stood behind the service counter, the restaurant itself looked a little neglected. Several customers searched for an empty place where they could sit, but they were understandably reluctant to sit at an unkempt table.

With a sigh of understanding, Dana stood up and began clearing the tables the staff hadn't been able to reach. Plates, trays, cutlery, and plenty of assorted crumbs graced far too many tables and booths. In addition, many nearly empty cups of coffee, juice, and milk added to the mess. Several minutes later, Dana glanced at the service counter, where several of the teenaged weekend employees engaged in friendly banter. Since no customers waited in line at the time, Dana signaled for a few workers to come out to the eating area.

Two girls approached with guilty looks on their faces, and Dana forced herself to remain calm. After all, they had done an excellent job serving the customers.

"Okay, guys," Dana said, smiling to relieve any tension. "You're doing a great job with the folks coming in. Nice attitudes, fast service, the works. I'm putting down good things in my report."

They appeared to relax as she spoke. "Thanks, Miss Edwards," said the girl who wore a name tag that said "Marcy."

"You can call me Dana," she told them, hoping to ease any remaining fears they might have. She knew what it felt like to

5

be a teenaged employee on the receiving end of a correction from the boss. "We do have a slight problem," she continued. "To be more specific, the eating area needs some TLC. You've got to find a balance here." She indicated the expanse of the room with her outstretched arm. "After receiving fast, pleasant service at the counter, the customers still need a clean place to sit down and eat their bagels or drink their coffee."

The girls nodded.

Dana pointed to a table behind them. "See that one right there? Now tell the truth. Would you eat at it?"

"Not really," said the other girl, shaking her head.

"Neither would I. I've been watching the customers, and they don't like the looks of it either," said Dana in a firm, but gentle, manner. "I want you guys to clean up what's out here right now. Is there some type of system to make sure things don't pile up like this when the place gets busy?"

The second girl shrugged, while Marcy shook her head, indicating the answer was no. "Kim keeps reminding us, but we forget sometimes."

Dana made a mental note to include this issue in her talk with Kim, the store's full-time manager. "I understand," she told the girls. "But something more will have to be done. I'll talk to Kim and see if we can't come up with a workable solution. Remember, Grady Bakeries are a family-owned business, and Mr. and Mrs. Grady want their customers to know that even though we have two new locations, the quality of service they've enjoyed since the first store opened will not be compromised."

"Okay," said Marcy. "We'll try to do better."

"Good. Thanks for cooperating." Dana returned to her table. She gathered her notebooks and purse, then went back to the kitchen. Hopefully Kim had finished receiving and inventorying an early morning shipment of supplies so they could have a short meeting before Dana had to get to the next store.

On her way to the back, she refilled her coffee mug. The past week had been a blur, consisting of a never ending series of driving back and forth among the three locations of the Grady Bakery stores to observe operations. This morning, she had rolled out of bed at five o'clock in order to get here by six, and at eight A.M., her energy reserves were dwindling rapidly.

Dana inhaled deeply, energized by the scent. The coffee made the often long hours she worked more pleasant. Grady Bakeries had great blends, and she loved walking into one of the stores first thing in the morning to be greeted with the heavy aroma of gourmet brew.

As she rounded the corner, she nearly ran into Kim, who hurried out from the back. "Whoa!" Dana tried not to spill the contents of her mug.

Kim grinned. "Whoops, sorry."

"It's okay." The mug had only been half-full, so she hadn't lost a drop.

"The last thing I want to do in the middle of a performance review is spill the boss's coffee." Kim laughed. "Especially a boss who we all know *needs* her morning coffee."

"You're right about that," Dana added, teasing her good friend and coworker. She and Kim had previously worked together here at the original bakery location, where Dana had been the manager, and Kim, the assistant manager.

When Mr. and Mrs. Grady opened the two new stores six months earlier, the two women received promotions; Kim, as the manager of this first location in the small city of Clayton and Dana, as the general manager of operations for all three stores.

"Your hair looks so cute. I love the French twist," Kim said while they walked back to the office.

"Thanks. I spent twelve hours getting it braided last week. Sitting in that chair feels like torture sometimes, but it works for me in the long run. All I have to do at night is wrap them. In the morning, I either wear them down or put them up, like today."

"I'm thinking of getting braids this summer," said Kim. "You'll have to give me your stylist's number."

"No problem. My sister Latrice does them. She's the family hair artist."

"I'll definitely give her a call then. Now, about the review. . . how did we do? Or do you have time right now? What's your schedule like for the rest of the day?"

Dana glanced out of the big windows that lined the front of the store. The recent weather in the St. Louis area had been unpredictable. Several storms blanketed the city in nearly a foot of snow, though the streets were now clear. Right now, a smattering of flakes gently fell from clouds that promised even more snow, and Dana knew maneuvering through traffic might prove to be difficult. Glancing at her watch, she told Kim, "I think we can go over a few things, but I need to be at the Kirkwood store from ten 'til two."

Kim shrugged. "You've got plenty of time. Kirkwood is only twenty minutes away."

"On a good day, but with this snow and traffic, I'll have to add another ten minutes to the drive."

Kim laughed. "That's right. I forgot you drive like my grandmother." She led the way to her office, and Dana followed.

The small, brightly lit room felt much warmer and cozier than the rooms in other parts of the building. Dana thought of her own office above the new store in the city of Creve Coeur and sighed. In the six months since she'd taken her new job, and the accompanying office, she hadn't done a thing to beautify her workspace. The walls remained a generic, new-construction white, and the only furniture items were her desk, chair, and file cabinets. In a word, the room felt and looked bland, and she really disliked being there.

Kim, on the other hand, had taken a nondescript room and infused it with color. She'd painted the walls a cozy yellow and stuffed warmth into every nook and cranny, using colorful accents and figurines, along with a green-and-gold area rug. The crowning jewels of this space were the overstuffed armchairs Kim bought for a song at a garage sale. Kim always had an eye for potential and expertly reupholstered the chairs herself, using colorfully patterned chenille. If jealousy weren't sinful, Dana might easily be quite envious about Kim's beautiful office and her natural gift for interior decoration.

"It's eight o'clock now, and you have about an hour and a half before you need to leave for Kirkwood," Kim announced once they were seated. "So tell me your initial thoughts. How did my folks do out there during the rush?"

Dana began a detailed report of what she witnessed and pointed out small glitches and major problems, including the table mess problem. Kim dutifully took notes, and she and Dana spent a good length of time dialoguing about how to fix things.

At nine fifteen, Kim glanced at the clock on the wall. "Well, we've got a lot to work on, but don't worry about my staff. We'll have things going smoother in no time."

"I know you will, and I'll be sure to tell that to the Gradys when I meet with them tonight," Dana promised.

Kim leaned back in her reclining armchair. "You have a meeting with them tonight?"

As Dana nodded, a now familiar sense of worry momentarily gripped her. Hoping Kim hadn't noticed her sudden change in demeanor, Dana forced a big smile and changed the subject, "So, what's new with you?"

"Uh-uh." Kim shook her head. "I saw that look on your face. What's going on with the Gradys that you don't want me to know about?"

"Nothing," Dana replied in a firm voice.

Kim's eyes narrowed. "Dana, I know you. We've worked together for two years. Something is wrong, and it's about work. Am I right?" She paused, then added, "You don't have to pretend with me. Everyone is talking about it."

Dana let out a resigned sigh. "Okay. Yes. I mean, no. Actually, I don't know, but I have a feeling I might find out soon."

Kim tapped her pencil on the edge of the desk, a habit Dana had often seen surface whenever her friend grew nervous. Kim stared across the room for a moment, then looked back to her. "I know the Gradys are concerned about profit since the new stores have opened. Craig, the manager at the Kirkwood store mentioned he heard Mr. Grady say he had some regrets about moving so quickly. Is that what's really going on?"

Dana pursed her lips, considering what she *could* say. Finally, she admitted, "I am aware of some financial concerns."

Fear marked Kim's expression. "Are we going to lose our jobs? Are they going to close the stores?"

"That's the last thing they want to do. But that's also why I've been reviewing procedure at the stores so carefully this month. Of course they expected to lose money after opening two brand-new stores. Still, they are pretty concerned about the figures they're seeing. Hopefully, after tonight's meeting, we'll have some kind of preliminary solutions. I have some ideas I've been thinking over that I'd like to discuss with them."

"I hope so," Kim remarked. "I just bought a new car. I really can't afford to lose my job."

"Same here. My car isn't all that reliable, but I've been waiting to buy something newer until I have more answers."

"My mortgage payment isn't all that cheap either," said Kim. "I mean, my two sisters and I split the bill three ways, but it wouldn't be a picnic if one of us couldn't pay for a few months. If I get fired or laid off, it'll affect them until I can find another job."

The alarm on Dana's watch went off, indicating the time had come for her to head to her next stop for the day. She gave Kim an apologetic nod. "I know; it's a little scary. But pray. And pray hard. This will get worked out."

Kim walked Dana back down the hallway, through the kitchen, and out to the public area of the bakery. "Drive carefully, and call me as soon as you know anything."

"Don't worry, I will. I won't see the Gradys until this evening around six, so I might end up calling you tomorrow."

"That's fine."

Dana opened the door and waved good-bye to Kim. As she walked to the car, she wrapped her scarf around her neck to form a more effective shield from the icy cold winds. She hurried the last few steps to her car and waited a few minutes for the engine to warm up. On her way to the next store, her thoughts were troubled. When it snowed, she usually enjoyed looking at the scenery, but today she couldn't seem to find much joy in the steady sifting of fluffy snowflakes. Kim's concerns were valid, and many others in the company shared the same fears.

Grady Bakeries were in serious financial trouble, and so far, there hadn't been any plausible antidotes. Dana needed to entertain the very real possibility that her job could be in jeopardy. The idea was a scary one, not only for her—with the opening of the two new stores, the Gradys had tripled their employee base, and many of those workers were adults with families who counted on the paychecks and benefits they received.

Dana thought about Kim's comments and knew many others would have trouble making their car or house payments. A feeling of relief washed over Dana because she had waited to shop for a new car until after her work situation became more stable. She had given up her apartment to lease a small house which belonged to the Gradys. They had given her a more than generous deal. In the event that they would have to raise the rent or cut her salary, Dana doubted she would find a better bargain, but she could probably move in with her parents for awhile.

Dana pulled the car to a stop at a red light and briefly closed her eyes to pray. "Lord, please send the Gradys some help. I want to keep my job, but I don't want to see others lose their jobs, and I don't want the Gradys to lose the company they've been building for almost thirty years. I know it's all in Your hands, so I'm praying that You would be merciful to all of the people who are depending on this company for their livelihoods."

## *two*

At the next store, Dana definitely sensed low morale. When he saw her come into the store, Craig, who stood behind the counter talking to one of the employees, motioned for Dana to go on back to his office.

Dana took a short detour to the coffeepot for some of the warm brew and headed toward the office to wait for Craig. A few minutes later, he came in. At only eight past ten in the morning, Craig looked tired and didn't seem to be his usual happy-go-lucky self.

Dana pasted on a smile and tried to sound positive. "Looks pretty busy out there. Has it been like that all morning?"

He shook his head. "Unfortunately, no. Things just picked up about ten minutes ago. I had seven people scheduled to come in at six o'clock, and things were so slow, I sent three of them home at nine. I hated to do it, but we were just bumping into each other with nothing to do."

Dana sat down in one of the chairs facing Craig's desk. "I don't understand how this can be happening. When we had just the one store in Clayton, we never seemed to have a lull in activity. Now, the traffic pattern is pretty sketchy. All three stores are getting a minimal number of customers. What's going on?"

Craig made a mumbling sound and began digging through his desk drawers. He pulled out a shiny, colorful flyer and handed it to Dana. "This is what the problem is. They're taking our customers."

Dana grabbed the paper and took a good look at it. The ad

13

touted the virtues of a new bakery called The Loaf, and although she had seen their flyers and advertisements before, she hadn't paid much attention to them. She shook her head. "I don't think so. People love our bakery. Who can resist wholesome organic baked goods that have been well known in the community for twenty-six years?"

With a guilty look on his face, Craig pointed to a half-eaten muffin resting on his desk. "Even loyal customers have short memories when certain stores have Banana Macadamia Mania Muffins and we don't."

Feeling shocked, Dana glanced from the muffin, to Craig, then back to the muffin. There were no "rules" preventing Grady employees from eating food from other stores, but the idea that Craig had brought food from a competitor's store *into* a Grady bakery unsettled her. "That's not one of ours?" She examined it more closely.

He grimly shook his head. "Don't get me wrong—I like our food, but I thought I'd do a little research. You know, scope out the competition." He shrugged. "To be honest, I actually bought the first one a couple of weeks ago. I know it doesn't look very loyal, so I'm trying to break the habit."

Dana couldn't think of a word to say. She'd come for a routine performance review, only to meet a manager confessing he loved the competitor's muffins. She opened her mouth, then closed it, deciding that this definitely qualified as one of those times when less was more.

Craig suddenly snatched up the remaining portion of the muffin and tossed it into the trash can, looking very proud of himself. "There," he said, shaking his hands emphatically. "I'm sorry. It won't happen again."

Dana cleared her throat, wondering how the day could take a turn for the bizarre at such an early hour. She took off her coat and placed it over the back of the chair, then stood. "I think I need a refill on this coffee. I'll run out front to grab some, then we can discuss operations when I come back."

Craig nodded, his gaze drifting toward the trash can. "Okay, I'll wait for you," he said.

Dana grimaced while she walked to the coffee machine. The way Craig had eyed that trash can, she wondered if other customers felt the same way about that new bakery. When she returned, Craig seemed much more like his normal self. He sipped from a glass of water, and he had several folders out on the desk for Dana to review.

"Well," she said, taking a seat again. "You know how these reviews go. I check all of your review files, and I need to sit and observe how things are going from the customers' point of view. Before I head out there, are there any things that really concern you about business in general?"

"For one thing, I'm hearing all kinds of rumors that the Gradys are going to shut us down." He stopped, then nodded. "Yeah. That concerns me. If they're closing the stores, I need to know now. We're a single-income family, and my wife home schools our kids, so I don't want her to work."

Dana nodded in agreement. "I know how you feel, and I've been hearing rumors over at the corporate office myself. Unfortunately, I don't have any definite answers. There are problems, but the Gradys don't want to close the stores. I have a meeting with them tonight, and we'll hopefully get to discuss it. I have several ideas I think could help turn things around."

"Okay. But if it looks like things are getting bad, I'm telling you I want out as soon as possible. I know the bakery business well, and The Loaf is hiring managers. If things are going sour here, I'd like to make a fairly quick transition."

Dana blinked. "You had an interview with them?"

"Not yet. Exactly. But it's only fair to me and my family, you know?"

"Of course." Dana leaned back in her chair, thinking. Maybe the lagging sales at Grady stores had more to do with that new bakery than she had allowed herself to believe. "Okay, Craig. You think The Loaf is taking our customers. Tell me why."

Craig didn't hesitate before he answered. "Dana, our food is good, but it's, well. . .old. It's not exciting. Customers are fickle, and the menu at The Loaf is interesting." He shrugged. "I can't entirely blame the customers. Everything on our menu sounds. . .boring." He winced. "Did that sound too harsh?"

Dana frowned. His comments were far more blunt than she had expected, yet his honesty made her respect him that much more.

"No, no," she said, shaking her head. "In fact, I'm glad you told me. These are things I'll need to discuss with the Gradys tonight. I'm sure they are aware of The Loaf, but it's good to have input from your perspective as well. This could be an important factor in what they decide to do."

Craig sighed, looking relieved. He ran his hands through his sandy blond hair, rumpling it. "Um. . .you know, if you do tell the Gradys, would you mind keeping me anonymous? I do like my job here, and if they don't close things down, I don't want them upset with me."

Dana laughed. "Craig, your muffin revelations startled me, but I know the Gradys well. They go to my church, and they're nice people. They are also very business minded, so they *want* to know things like this. They're not going to fire you for telling them how you feel."

"Good." He leaned back, looking satisfied. "Then you can use my name."

"Thank you." Before Dana could say more, the phone rang, and when he answered, one of the store's suppliers instantly drew him into a conversation that looked to be lengthy. He cupped his hand over the receiver and mouthed, "This won't take long."

Dana waved her hands to show that she didn't need to talk to him at the moment. "I'll take these papers and go and set up out front," she whispered. "When I'm done, I'll come back to talk with you."

He nodded and waved back, still carrying on with his phone conversation. Dana grabbed her coffee and headed to the dining room, where she spent the next two hours silently observing and taking notes about what she saw. Afterwards, she reviewed her findings with Craig for another half hour before leaving for her last review at the remaining store.

As she drove, she grew increasingly concerned about the competition. Why hadn't she paid more attention to The Loaf four months earlier when they first entered the market? "I could have at least gone in and checked them out," she muttered to herself.

The seed of an idea took root and rapidly grew. Maybe she *should* stop by one of their stores and take a look. Dana shook her head, even though she only argued with herself. It just didn't seem right. "I am a manager, not a spy."

Then again, what could it hurt? She had as a much of a right as anyone else to stop at a bakery and look at the menu. Realizing that she could get to one of the stores in under five minutes, Dana acted on impulse and decided to go ahead and pay The Loaf a visit.

Feeling very much like the key player in an espionage film, Dana circled the crowded parking lot several times before finally taking a space far away from the front door. She had two reasons for doing so; the first being she would be completely mortified if someone she knew recognized her car, and second, because no other spaces were available. The latter offered her no comfort, and she considered fleeing the scene; but her curiosity had been tickled, and she simply had to find out what kind of magnet behind those doors consistently pulled in such large crowds.

She quickly made her way through the cold air to take shelter indoors. She pulled open the massive, eggplant-colored doors and instantly relaxed after catching a whiff of the decidedly cozy aroma of baked goods and brewing coffee.

The long line snaked down the length of the counter, toward the door, and spilled into the eating area. The bright, modern décor matched perfectly with the lively music playing over the intercom and the cheery rumble of voices in the background.

Part of her felt like a traitor, but the more decisive part of her needed to stay and see what they were selling. Several people came in behind her, and since she hadn't exactly gotten in line yet, they rushed ahead of her to secure a spot in the long line.

Dana reluctantly edged closer to the back of the queue, wondering how long this would take. She had already sacrificed her lunch hour to come here, and she hated the idea that this trip might spill over into her working hours. She couldn't, in good conscience, visit this place on company time. Dana stopped and looked at her watch, noticing that one o'clock lurked around the corner, poised to make an appearance in less than ten minutes. Her lunch break officially lasted for an hour, but since Dana rarely even left the office for lunch, she decided that today she would splurge a little and stick this out.

Before she could take another step closer to the back of the line, another man swooshed past her and got in place. These people were serious about their bread, Dana decided, hurrying to get behind the man before someone else got in front of her.

While she waited, Dana looked around. Built very recently,

the interior of the store still sparkled. The two new Grady bakeries had never boasted such a high-gloss look, not even at their grand openings. They were clean and new, but the décor much more simple and the atmosphere far quieter. Dana had always liked the look of the Grady bakeries, but now she wondered if the simple, charming look had been a major mistake.

The man in front of her seemed to be doing a great deal of rubbernecking as well, and Dana wondered if the place awed him as much as it had her.

She studied him as he glanced around. He seemed vaguely familiar, but she couldn't be sure if she had seen him before or just known someone who looked like him. His appearance was not incredibly spectacular, but he did seem to stand out.

He towered at least ten inches over her height of five feet two. He had medium-toned skin and a short haircut. Dana had seen probably a million other men with similar features. What caught her attention about this man was his clothing. He dressed impeccably. The long, black overcoat he wore seemed almost an exact match to the one she and her sister-in-law, Stacy, bought for her brother, Max, this past Christmas—a single-breasted cashmere blend that turned out to be a great deal pricier than she or Stacy expected it to be.

Moments later, the stranger unbuttoned the coat and loosened the long cashmere scarf wrapped around his neck. Dana caught a glimpse of his ensemble, which consisted of a turtleneck, a charcoal blazer, and matching slacks.

A small sigh escaped her lips. She had never considered herself to be picky about a man's outward appearance. She always assumed that she would most likely end up with someone average looking who got dressed up like this no more than ten times after their wedding, but she suddenly realized

BEULAH BAPTIST CHURCH LIBRARY

there was something to be said about a man in a suit. *Something positive, that is.*

The man smiled down at her. Dana quickly shifted her gaze away, embarrassed to be caught staring. The line moved forward at a good pace, and she prayed it would move faster. In her peripheral vision, she could see him watching her, and she felt somewhat uncomfortable.

As she took a few more steps forward, she allowed herself another peek at the man. Even though his looks were average, he had a nice profile with his sculpted jawline, strong forehead, and well-shaped nose.

*Stop it!* she told herself. *No one pays any attention to things like that. Leave the descriptions to people who write novels.* The man glanced at her again, and Dana looked away, feeling ridiculous. *Stop overacting,* she chided herself.

*Maybe because the men I work with rarely ever put on a dress shirt, let alone an ensemble like this guy.* The bakery business could hardly be called a pristine, easy job. Though many of the people she worked with were men, whenever she saw them, they generally seemed to wear some of the baking ingredients. . .mostly flour.

Dana couldn't imagine this guy setting foot in a kitchen, unless he wanted to tell his kitchen staff what he'd like for dinner. He definitely looked like the type of man who'd have servants and maybe a manor on a hill somewhere. Someplace grand like. . .like where? A Mediterranean villa or a Caribbean mansion? *Nah. . .not this guy. He'd live somewhere like. . .*She tilted her head to the side and considered. Finally, she had an answer.

"Pemberley," she blurted out. For some reason, he reminded her of Mr. Darcy, from the Jane Austen novel. She didn't know if he might be as conceited as the infamous Mr. Darcy, but he certainly had a stately demeanor that reminded her of the character. Unfortunately, she had neglected to confine her imaginative thoughts to her mind, where no one else would hear them.

"Excuse me?" the man asked, turning around to face her.

# three

Dana's throat went dry. How could she have allowed herself to say something so. . .silly . . .and fictional? And out loud, at that. Pemberley, the home of Mr. Darcy, didn't really exist outside of Jane Austen's novel, *Pride & Prejudice*.

The man, still waiting for her to answer, cleared his throat softly. "Did you say something?"

"No," she answered quickly, feeling her face grow warm. She couldn't tell a lie. "I mean, yes. But I was just talking to myself."

"Oh," he said, lifting his eyebrows. "If that gets too boring, you can always just talk to me. I don't think I would be terrible company, and the conversation wouldn't be one sided."

Dana smiled politely in an attempt to collect every remaining ounce of her dignity and to refrain from leaving the store immediately.

"So, do you come here often?" he asked, seemingly determined to embarrass her further.

"Do you?" She hated answering questions posed to her by strangers.

He shook his head. "Actually, I'm new in town. Just transferred here for a job. I hoped you might be willing to tell me your favorite things on the menu."

*Ah ha!* Dana thought. He was a new customer as well. She should probably try to win him over to Grady Bakeries. "I never come here," she said matter-of-factly. "I usually get all my baked goods at another place."

He looked amused. "So if you never come here, why are you here. . .now?"

Dana took a deep breath. Obviously, he was one of those people who took everything literally, but he did it in a rather charming way. "I guess I just wanted to check out what they have. Thought I'd try something new, but now I don't know. . . ." Dana paused and shook her head. Craning her neck to look toward the front of the line, she sighed. "It doesn't even seem like this stop will be worth it. If we don't start moving, I'll go to my usual bakery."

"You have my attention now," he said. "Tell me about the other place."

"Oh," Dana waved her hand dismissively. "I know you've heard of it. Grady Bakeries? They serve excellent food, and they've been a part of the community for years and have three different locations." He didn't look very convinced about the virtues of Grady Bakeries so she continued. "Now this place here, The Loaf, it's only been open a few months. And you know how that can be. They could just be a fad, a flash in the pan. They might not last the year." She tried to look sympathetic.

He grinned. "I doubt it, judging from the crowd here. They have plenty of customers, but if what you said is true, it's a good thing you came here before they start boarding up the windows and trying to sell the place. Otherwise, you might never know what you missed."

Dana fought the urge to frown. She felt absolutely childish trying to convince even *one* customer to stop visiting this place. If he wanted to shop here, she had no power to stop him.

"But," he said, "I'm planning to check out that other store you mentioned while I'm in town."

"Good. I think you'll probably like it." Not bothering to hide her curiosity, she asked, "So where are you from?"

He shook his head. "Most recently, I'm from New Jersey, but that's just the latest stop in the string of places I've lived.

I'm originally from New York, but I'm in St. Louis for a job interview."

"So you'll be moving here?"

He nodded. "I think so. I have a meeting tonight with my potential employers, but I think I have things pretty well set." He winked. "From what I can tell, I think they need my help."

Part of Dana felt a tad irked by his extreme confidence, which she felt bordered on an over-inflated ego; but at the same time, she began rapidly accumulating a list of questions about him. She wanted to ask his name, what type of work he did, and where he had lived before New Jersey, but she held her tongue in check.

Beyond what he had told her, she knew nothing about him, and if she started asking too many questions, he would probably feel slighted if she didn't reciprocate with information about herself. She didn't feel comfortable giving out so many of her own personal details to a total stranger.

They were very close to the front of the line now, and Dana lifted her gaze to examine the menu, hopefully, in order to put an end to their conversation. While he seemed nonthreatening, and she didn't feel afraid of him, she knew she couldn't be too trusting. He seemed to take the hint that she didn't want to keep talking and turned around.

Next in line, he stepped up to the counter to place his order. He had a melodic but deep voice, and he spoke articulately. He also proceeded to request one of nearly everything on the menu.

Dana wondered what in the world he would do with all of that food. Not only did he buy loaves of bread, but in addition, he got cookies, pastries, and bagels. Maybe he was shopping for a party.

Realizing that she was staring at him again, Dana forced herself to concentrate on the menu. Overwhelmed by the wide array of options, she didn't know what to choose. When one of the people behind the counter called on her, she stepped up and ordered a loaf of wheat bread and a Chocolate Raisin Oatmeal Buddy muffin. She didn't know why she picked those two items, but she felt a tremendous amount of pressure to not hold up the line when she'd had nearly fifteen minutes to make her decision.

When the clerk handed her the bag, Dana quickly paid for the items and headed to the door. So much for espionage, she thought. How in the world had she picked such mundane items? When she reached the exit, she noticed that the man from the line followed directly behind her. If he hadn't looked threatening before, he appeared even more harmless now, with his arms full of bags of bread.

Since he would probably have a hard enough time getting his car unlocked, Dana held the door open for him.

"Thanks," he said.

"No problem."

They walked silently for a few more steps until he reached his car, parked conveniently close to The Loaf's front door. He put several of the bags on the hood while he got his keys, while Dana continued toward her own car. "Hey!" he called.

She turned around to see what he wanted.

"I don't know your name."

She shrugged helplessly. "Sorry, but I don't feel comfortable giving you that kind of information. I don't know you."

He looked disappointed. "Okay," he said slowly. "What if I tell you my name?"

She considered it for a minute. She really didn't know this guy, and as much as she might like to get acquainted, she heard warning signals going off in her head—signals that sounded exactly like her parents and seven overprotective siblings. The baby of her family, Dana had been a very outgoing child—so outgoing that her parents feared for her safety sometimes, due to her tendency to strike up conversations with complete strangers.

Her five brothers and two sisters, ever vigilant and highly bossy, had taken it upon themselves to serve as Dana's acting parents when their parents weren't around.

Unfortunately, her siblings, not being *parents*, did not approach these warnings with the same tact and gentle firmness with which her parents had. Their method of choice had been to frighten Dana with images and stories of the worst possible things that could happen to her. Of course, this had been very convincing to her as a young child, but still to this day, she sometimes got nervous chills when she met people in uncontrolled environments, outside of places like church or work.

Like now. She shook her head. "Sorry, I don't think so."

He looked even more disappointed, and Dana considered granting his request. After all, telling him her name hardly compared to giving out state secrets.

Before she could answer, he brightened. "Maybe I'll see you at that other bakery."

"Maybe," she said cautiously.

"Any chance you might tell me which one you usually go to?"

Dana grinned. This, she could handle. If he came to the bakery, she would feel more secure in that environment—on her own turf, so to speak. "I go to all three."

He nodded. "Then I'll be on the lookout for you."

"I'll be on the lookout for you too." She hurried to her car because the wind made it way too difficult to just stand around talking. If she ever saw this guy again, the Lord would have to arrange the details.

❧

Dana left the office early in order to go home and freshen up before her dinner meeting with the Gradys. She also sampled the muffin she'd gotten at The Loaf. Actually, the people at The Loaf had elevated the pastry above mere muffin status by naming it the Chocolate Raisin Oatmeal Buddy. Dana couldn't understand the name, but then again, the entire menu had been riddled with odd phrases and combinations. The muffin itself felt cold and hard from sitting out in the car for hours, but she remedied that by microwaving it.

Sitting at her tiny kitchen table, Dana cautiously nibbled the first bite. As she chewed and swallowed, she realized Craig had been right. Absolutely right. The Loaf had excellent muffins. As much as she hated to admit it, their muffins were far tastier than the ones sold at Grady Bakeries.

Dana's stomach churned, and she put the muffin down. If their muffins were this good, the rest of their bakery items could probably walk circles around the stuff sold in Grady stores. Dana reached for her cordless phone and dialed Kim's number.

Kim answered and sounded hesitant when she realized Dana waited on the line. "Is this about work? I just got home five minutes ago, and I wanted to have a long soak in the tub. You don't want to know what happened with me and a batch of sourdough starter five minutes before we closed."

Dana instantly envisioned several scenarios, all of them equally sticky. "Sorry. I just wanted to ask you something."

"Go ahead but be quick. Besides, don't you have a meeting tonight with the Gradys?"

"Yeah, and that's why I'm calling." Dana paused, wondering how she should proceed. Since Kim said she had little time, Dana decided not to beat around the bush and just ask the question. "Have you ever bought anything from The Loaf?"

Kim kept silent.

Dana waited.

Kim said nothing.

Dana cleared her throat. This felt like a replay of her discussion with Craig this morning. "Kim, this isn't an interrogation. I'm not going to fire you for buying something from them."

Kim let out a sigh. "Okay. Listen, this is what happened: My sisters brought home some Danishes once, the Cherry Cream Cheese Caper."

"The what?"

"Don't ask. All of their food has long names."

"Oh, don't get me started on the names," Dana said. "I bought a chocolate chip muffin, and I nearly ran out of breath trying to recite the name while I ordered it."

"So you go there too?" Before Dana could answer, Kim continued. "I'm glad to hear this from you. I felt like such a traitor because after we ate the Danishes, I went back to get more and discovered those Dill Fennel Drama baguettes. They're terrific with tuna salad. And now I feel much better knowing that you go too." Her words spilled out in a rush, "I guess I'm just tired of eating our stuff at work. It doesn't have the same pizzazz. I go to The Loaf almost every day to pick up something, and I've tasted pretty much everything they sell. So," Kim slowed down, "what's your favorite?"

"Um. Well, I don't know. I've never been there before today," Dana said pointedly.

"Oh. I see. This was a trap, huh? You got me to spill my guts about my secret trips to the other bakery so you can tell on me at your meeting?"

Dana shook her head, even though Kim couldn't see her. "No, that's not it. I've been wrapped up in my work and hadn't realized our competition is formidable until this morning when Craig mentioned it. I went there this afternoon and bought a couple of things."

"So what do you think?"

"I think we're in trouble," Dana said without hesitation.

"You just said we couldn't get fired for eating at another bakery. Why the sudden change?"

"No, not 'we' as in our jobs. At least not right now," Dana admitted. "But I think The Loaf is a big reason that our business has been down."

"I know," Kim said. "To think—I've been chipping away at my own job by eating stuff from that place. I promise I won't go back. Not even for one of those Cilantro Parmesan Peace bagels. I won't let my sisters go either. You can count on it."

"Thanks, but that's too little, too late. Even if none of our workers shop there, people will still go in droves. We have to do something, and I plan to talk to the Gradys about this tonight."

"Good. We do need to do something. They've had the same menu since the bakery opened, and I was a little kid then. We need change."

Dana didn't think that qualified as the solution. "There's something to be said for classic simplicity, Kim. I don't think we need to go out and copy The Loaf's menu."

"Copy? No," Kim agreed. "Update? Yes, yes, a thousand times yes."

"I never thought I would hear someone who likes antiques criticize something for being *old*," Dana quipped.

"Classic simplicity is great for furniture but a waste of time and money when it comes to the food business. People want new and exciting, and if you don't give it to them, they go where the action is."

Dana still didn't agree, but she decided not to make an issue of it. She would take her concerns to the Gradys, and since they had developed the first menu, she felt sure they would see her point. They needed more publicity right away.

The menu wasn't as hip as the one over at The Loaf, but trends were always coming and going. Grady Bakeries had the benefit of time and experience on their side, and Dana remained confident they would prevail in the end. To Kim, she said, "We'll see what the Gradys think."

"Good idea. I'll be praying," Kim assured her. "Call me when you know something. I'm on pins and needles about this."

"Me too. I've got to run and get ready for dinner, but I'll probably be sending out a memo Monday morning."

"Or, you could just call me tonight. It's not like I'll be asleep or anything. Who can sleep when her job is up in the air?"

"Okay," Dana agreed. "If it's not too late, I'll call you tonight."

"Define your idea of 'too late.' I have a feeling we have differing opinions on the matter," Kim persisted.

"Kim. . ." Dana said. "Just let me go and get ready, okay?"

"All right."

Dana hung up and went to her closet to decide out what she would wear for her dinner meeting. Since they were dining at a small, somewhat formal place, she decided on a black matte jersey tunic with a matching pair of comfortable pants.

She flipped open her compact of pressed powder, ran the sponge over her face a couple of times, then applied a quick touch of mascara, put on a touch of the deep reddish lipstick she saved for special occasions, and grabbed her coat.

❧

The restaurant was located in downtown Clayton, only ten minutes away from her bungalow in Richmond Heights, but the temperature had dropped, and she didn't want to speed on roads that might possibly be a little slippery. Dana arrived ten minutes early, just as Mr. and Mrs. Grady were arriving.

Mrs. Grady got out as soon as her husband stopped the car. She made a beeline toward Dana and ushered her into the restaurant. "It's too cold to stand out here talking." They waited inside the doorway for Mr. Grady, then were led to their table.

As soon as they were seated, Dana reached into her over-sized shoulder bag and pulled out the notebook she'd been carrying around.

Mr. Grady took one look at the book and shook his head. He gently took it, closed the cover, and set it aside. "Let's at least order appetizers first."

"Besides, Ethan isn't here yet," said Mrs. Grady.

Dana looked from Mrs. Grady to her husband. "Who's Ethan?"

Mr. Grady smiled. "Let's order something, then I'll explain."

Dana didn't feel very hungry, but Mr. Grady made it clear that he wanted to eat soon, so business matters would have to wait for a bit. They discussed the weather until the waiter arrived with iced tea and a platter of portabella mushrooms stuffed with a cream cheese and crab mixture.

After a few bites of mushroom, Mr. Grady glanced around the room, looking worried. "I wonder what's keeping Ethan so long?" Patting his wife's hand, he added, "We should have stopped by his hotel and driven him over."

Mrs. Grady nodded. "He must have gotten lost."

Mr. Grady looked at Dana. "I guess you're ready to talk business. Why don't you tell me how the reviews went today?"

Dana agreed and began her narrative of how things had gone. She concluded with a lengthy statement concerning the competition from The Loaf.

To her surprise, Mr. and Mrs. Grady not only agreed but also indicated they were well on the way to finding a remedy for the problem.

Mrs. Grady sighed. "I guess our menu is a little dated, but

until The Loaf opened, people seemed to like what we were selling. Now, we have no choice but to make some rather extensive changes."

Dana wrinkled her forehead. She had already indicated to Kim that she felt Grady Bakeries could make a recovery without trying to copy The Loaf's strategy, but it didn't appear that the Gradys felt the same as she did. "What do you mean by changes?" Dana ventured cautiously.

Mr. Grady grinned. "We're going to give our entire menu a makeover," he said, speaking in low tones, as though the competition sat at the next table.

"The whole menu?" Dana asked, shocked. She loved that menu. Solid and dependable, it never changed, and Dana felt its real beauty lay in true simplicity. "How?"

"We're hiring someone who knows what people really want," said Mr. Grady. "And you're going to help him."

Mrs. Grady clasped her hands together, looking excited. "His name is Ethan Miles, and he's a very experienced chef. He's lived all over the world, so he knows all of the latest trends."

Dana blinked. They were trying to get ahead by copying the competition and somehow needed her to lend a hand in all of this. She shook her head. "But I'm not a baker. I'm not even part of the marketing department. I'm just the general manager. How am I going to help?"

"You're going to be Ethan's assistant," Mr. Grady said. "I am spending a great deal of money to revitalize our image. He will need someone to introduce him to the workers, get him acclimated to the city, and help him go over the records to analyze what items sell best. You'll also have to help organize product development and testing, then help the stores integrate the new items and phase out the old as seamlessly as possible."

Dana couldn't talk. Her job currently devoured more overtime hours than she preferred to count, and now Mr. Grady had essentially suggested she work the equivalent of two jobs. She did her best to hide her displeasure. She felt slighted that they hadn't asked her opinion before deciding to make her play secretary to an overpaid baker while doing her regular duties.

This was downright ridiculous! She began gathering ideas to voice her complaint, but before she could say anything, Mr. Grady stood up and beckoned someone over to the table. Dana sat with her back stiff, unwilling to acknowledge this troublemaker right away. She inhaled deeply, trying not to let her temper take over.

To put things simply, she felt wronged. She hadn't been shown the respect her position afforded her. She should have been a part of the decision-making process instead of having the news thrust on her five minutes before she met her new "boss." Normally, she took charge of things at work. She told the other employees what to do and answered directly to the Gradys and no one else—until now.

*"Learn to be a servant of all. . . ."* The words seemed no louder than a whisper, a glimmer of one of the Bible verses Dana had memorized as a little girl. She sighed, realizing the truth of the verse. In order to be great in God's kingdom, a person first needed to learn how to serve others, just like Jesus had. Still. . .it didn't feel good. She had always imagined that if she were ever in this position, it would somehow feel more noble. This didn't feel noble. It stung her pride. *"Pride goes before destruction, a haughty spirit before a fall."* The verse echoed in her ears. Dana closed her eyes.

*Okay, Lord,* she admitted. *I'm trying to learn what it is You're trying to teach me.* She opened her eyes and turned around to find herself facing the man from the line at The Loaf.

He smiled, almost as if he were amused to find her here.

"Dana," said her boss, "This is Ethan." Turning to Ethan, he said, "Ethan, this is—"

"Dana," Ethan said, interrupting him. To Dana, he said, "I didn't think I would find out your name this soon."

Dana blinked. She couldn't think of a single word to say, but she was well aware her three tablemates were waiting for her to comment.

# four

Suppressing a grin at Dana's sudden silence, Ethan picked up the conversation, explaining to the Gradys how he had run into Dana earlier at The Loaf. "I asked for her phone number, but she wouldn't give it to me."

"Dana is our operations manager, so you don't have to worry about her phone number. I imagine you'll see enough of each other at work," Mr. Grady supplied with a chuckle.

Ethan felt pleased. He'd had a sneaking suspicion earlier that the woman he'd met at the bakery might somehow be more than just a dedicated Grady Bakery customer. Smiling at the Gradys, Ethan added, "It's nice to know that I'll be working for a company whose employees are so *committed* to finding ways to win new customers."

Dana's eyes widened at his statement, and Ethan wondered if she thought he might be making fun of her.

She cleared her throat. "Well, I'm glad you're supposed to be the marketing genius. It seems that my plan to infiltrate the customer line at The Loaf would be far too time consuming." She gave him an overly sweet smile, then turned her attention to the menu.

Ethan tugged at his collar, feeling vaguely uncomfortable, as if he'd wandered into the midst of a battlefield while the opposing sides reloaded their weapons. The calm before the storm.

Resolving to keep quiet until he knew more about the situation, he grabbed his glass of ice water and quickly gulped down enough to give him a momentary headache.

Mr. Grady cleared his throat. "In our earlier conversations, you mentioned needing an assistant to help with your research and development."

Ethan nodded. "Yes, and you said that you didn't know if you had the finances to create another position so suddenly. Have you made any decisions either way?"

Mr. Grady nodded slowly, glancing across the table to Dana. She sat with her back as straight as a rod, her chin lifted high.

"I'm going to be your assistant," she informed him, her mouth forming a smile that didn't look very happy.

Now Ethan knew the origin of the problem he sensed. For reasons that remained unknown, while Dana had seemed interested in him personally, she didn't seem particularly thrilled with the idea of being his assistant. He hoped to prolong eye contact, but she once again turned her attention to her menu.

Just then, the waiter came around, ready to take orders. Ethan quickly decided on a pasta dish flavored with an herb and cream sauce.

While the rest of the table ordered, he thought about the situation with Dana. Should he tell the Gradys that he could do the job without her? If he did, where would that leave him? He *needed* an assistant. Of course, if absolutely necessary, he could do the job alone, but it would take longer and end up costing the Gradys more money.

Ethan wondered if Dana would get a pay increase to do this job and if she would still be expected to do her previous duties in addition to being his helper. She still remained very quiet, and Ethan had a feeling this new job had come as a surprise to her.

After the waiter left, Mr. Grady asked Ethan if he felt ready to give any details of his ideas for the company. Ethan relaxed somewhat. Talking about work seemed far more comfortable than wondering how to smooth things over with his new—and apparently unwilling—assistant.

He related what he bought and tasted from the menu at The Loaf. In the end, he concluded that their food boasted a new and exciting look and taste; he held no doubt that he could formulate a competitive menu for the Gradys.

Ethan explained his thoughts to the Gradys, then added, "But on Monday, I'd like to give your menu the same going over. I'm not quite convinced that we should have to throw everything out. If what you already sell has been successful this long, then maybe it's not totally done for. In my experience as a pastry chef, people are always looking for something new; yet, after the new has worn off, they tend to gravitate back to familiar favorites."

Dana seemed to perk up at this statement, and Ethan felt relieved that his image could be improving in her eyes. In his opinion, Dana's approval would be a good thing. After their initial meeting that afternoon, he'd been very disappointed that he'd not even learned so much as her name.

During the ride back to his hotel, Ethan had worked to burn her image into his memory. A petite, captivating beauty, Dana was the total package.

Her round cheeks, wide, velvety brown eyes, full lips that showcased pretty white teeth, and cassia-toned skin all combined to form the most memorable face Ethan had ever seen. Barely over five feet tall, she was built like a Normal Woman, with a capital N.

Ethan had realized he had no reason to be so concerned with remembering how she looked. To put things simply, Dana was unforgettable.

After mentally kicking himself for not finding a way to continue their conversation, Ethan's disappointment had threatened to cloud his entire day. After a good half hour of trying to figure out what he should have said and done to get more information, he'd given up and turned the whole issue over to the Lord. "If You want me to see her again, then I'm ready to let You arrange things," he had prayed.

Even though he had been sincere, he didn't expect much to come of his request. The sight of her this evening jolted him. Just as he'd been ready to conclude that the Lord did indeed want him and Dana to meet again, his excitement deflated after he encountered Dana's hesitance.

Now, instead of being enthusiastic, he felt confused. He wanted to tell the Gradys that he would do the job alone but then worried that Dana might feel he had belittled her ability to do the job—and he didn't want that to happen.

Was the fact that Dana would be working with him a mere coincidence, or did the Lord really have something more in mind?

❧

Dana felt out of kilter. Earlier this afternoon, this man seemed charming and attractive. Now, despite the fact that he hadn't really done anything to her, she fought the impression that he could almost be an enemy. *At least, not yet.* Already, she'd be forced to rearrange her work schedule in order to help him.

Dana glanced at Ethan, wondering what qualified him to succeed at this job. His appearance didn't seem to suggest he could resolve the situation. Dana considered his ensemble this afternoon to be quite dressy, but this evening, his attire appeared even more formal.

Wearing a black dinner jacket and matching pants along with the same cashmere coat and scarf, Ethan had made his entrance in the restaurant smelling of new clothes and looking as unwrinkled and glossy as a magazine photo. This image didn't mesh with Dana's image of the traditional chef.

In spite of her reservations, Dana couldn't deny that the opportunity to work with him did interest her. At least he didn't need to change everything. Perhaps, given the opportunity to work side by side with him, she could be influential enough to prevent him from disturbing too much of the company's foundation.

During the remainder of the meal, Ethan and the Gradys plotted and planned their new marketing schedule. Dana stared at her dinner and did her best to look cheerful, her feelings a strange jumble of expectation and dread. When the meal ended, she declined to stay for coffee and cheesecake and left early, pleading fatigue.

&

The weekend passed too quickly for Dana. After church on Sunday, she spent time with her family, who had gathered at her parent's home to celebrate her nephew's birthday.

Her mother noticed that something troubled Dana. After Dana finished explaining the situation, Mom didn't offer any direct advice.

"I think you'll have to decide what you need to do," said Mom. "Pride can be a tricky thing, and we have to be sure to react to a situation for the right reasons. Otherwise, we might let our own notions of how we should be treated take over and start to control us."

Dana pursed her lips. This wasn't the type of advice she'd hoped for. "Okay, I understand that, but don't you think the Gradys were a little unfeeling about this?"

Mom shrugged her shoulders, and Dana knew she didn't see this situation the same way. "Honey," Mom began, "I don't think the Gradys meant you any harm by asking you to work with Ethan. But I do know their business is in trouble, and without their business, you wouldn't have this job. I can't tell you what to do, but I think if I were in your shoes, I'd work as hard as I could to help the company—and my job."

Dana knew her mother spoke the truth, but she couldn't help feeling a little sorry for herself. Most everyone else in her family tended to side with Mom's point of view, and Dana felt herself growing more frustrated.

Sure, she needed to give her all to help the company; but somehow, she felt they weren't willing to give her as much as she planned to devote them.

Monday morning she arrived at work, her heart heavy with the realization that she would, indeed, have to do her best to stick this out. Still, she wasn't looking forward to the job. After filling up her mug of coffee, she trudged into her office, hoping to get a few minutes to brace herself for Ethan's arrival.

Instead, she found him sitting at her desk, apparently waiting for her to arrive. Dana stopped abruptly in the doorway, accidentally sloshing some of her coffee over the sides of the mug. "Ouch!" she exclaimed, as the hot liquid trickled over her fingers.

Ethan jumped up, grabbed the mug from her, and set it down on the corner of her desk. Before she could say a word, he took her hand and examined it. Too stunned and embarrassed to protest, Dana stood there.

As he checked over her fingers, Vanessa, from the marketing department, walked into the office. She stopped, her eyes widening at the sight of Ethan holding Dana's hand. Before Dana could explain, Vanessa backed away. "Sorry, I didn't mean to interrupt. It's nothing important, so I'll come back later."

Dana snatched her hand away from Ethan, who gave her an amused look. "No harm done," he said. "But if I were you, I'd run it under cold water for a bit."

Dana shot a glare at him and practically ran down the hallway after Vanessa. The last thing she needed was for the rest of her coworkers to get the idea that she and Ethan were. . . well, anything more than two people working on a plan to help the company.

She located Vanessa in the break room, putting butter on a bagel and chattering to other workers. When Dana entered the room, Vanessa suddenly hushed.

Dana wanted to groan. News could certainly travel fast. Gathering all of her dignity, she held up her injured hand, which still dripped convincingly with coffee. "I spilled my coffee," she informed the entire room.

A few people nodded their heads and made sympathetic sounds.

As she headed toward the wet bar in the corner, Dana kept talking. "Ethan said I should run cold water over it to make sure it'll be okay." No one said anything. Determined to nip any rumors in the bud, Dana made a big show of running cold water over her hand. When she finished, she went to the bagel box and grabbed one.

"So," she said to Vanessa, "what did you need to talk to me about?" Trying not to sound or look desperate, Dana split the bagel and slathered cream cheese over it.

Vanessa gave her a blank stare.

Dana sighed. "Remember, you were just in my office?"

A look of realization came over Vanessa's face. "Oh, that," she said. "I just wanted to check with you about some of the new ads we've been working on. Mr. Grady came in earlier. He said that before we run the new ads, we should check with you since we're going to be taking some things off of the menu."

Dana felt mildly pleased. At least Mr. Grady hadn't come in and announced to everyone that Ethan now ran the show. Suddenly, she frowned. Mr. Grady never came into the office before eleven—on the days he did come in to work. "Mr. Grady was already here this morning? Before I got here?"

Vanessa nodded. "He brought Chef Miles in and introduced him to everyone."

"Oh." Dana's heart sank a bit. She put the two halves of the bagel back together and lifted it to her mouth. Before she could take a bite, Vanessa held up a hand.

"Yes?" Dana asked, somewhat irritated.

Vanessa shrugged. "I thought you hated pumpernickel."

"I do."

Vanessa looked pointedly at the bagel Dana had just prepared.

Dana took a deep breath and looked at the piece of bread. Sure enough, she held a pumpernickel bagel. Dana wanted to groan. By now, everyone had gone back to quiet chatting, but they were still discreetly watching her.

Dana laughed nervously. Might there be any way to fix this without making herself look even sillier?

"Oh, pumpernickel—my favorite," said someone from behind her.

Dana didn't have to turn around to recognize that the voice belonged to Ethan. "Is this for me?" he asked, gesturing toward the bagel she held.

Dana shrugged. "If you want it."

"Thanks," he said, sounding really pleased. "I waited and waited for you to come back. How's the burn?"

"It's fine," Dana said firmly, moving away before he could grab it again. Now, everyone had dropped all pretense of conversation in order to watch the exchange.

He smiled. "Hey, this is a good system. I look over your scalded hand, and in return, you fix me a bagel. Think you could spill coffee every morning?"

Dana forced a smile. She supposed she could be happy that Ethan had just confirmed that she had, indeed, suffered a burn. However, that victory had been undone when he'd suggested to everyone within hearing that she had just skipped down to the break room to fix him breakfast.

Only about a tenth of all the employees were in the break room, but Dana knew how the account of her conversation with Ethan would travel once they left the room.

Rumors could spread around an office as quickly as news of a picnic moved through an anthill, and her efforts to quell any false ideas had probably only succeeded in furthering them.

Giving up on the idea of setting things right, Dana headed toward the doorway, while Ethan carried on a conversation with the others.

Before she could leave, she heard one of the women say, "Chef Miles, when do we *all* get to call you Ethan? Or do we have to be working directly with you for that privilege?"

Several others chuckled, and Dana winced, realizing she had made yet another mistake by using his first name when explaining about the burn.

Back at her office, she wearily sat down at her desk. She reached for her coffee, which now held an unappetizing chill. While she waited for Ethan to finish his breakfast, she alternated between wanting to laugh and cry. In some respects, this morning's incident might be funny, but right now, the humor wasn't all that prominent.

While trying to prepare for Ethan to return, she moved her coffee aside and tackled some paperwork she had left on Friday. She prayed that the menu issues could be resolved quickly so Ethan could go back to New York, and her life and job could return to normal; but in the back of her mind, Dana had a feeling she would be in this for the long haul.

*five*

"Hmm," Ethan mumbled, chewing yet another bite of bread. He swallowed and took a drink of water. Glancing at the platter in front of him, he took a deep breath and reached for another piece.

"What do you call this one?" he asked Dana, who sat across the table.

"Oatmeal wheat."

"Just oatmeal wheat?"

Dana lifted her eyebrows slightly. "That's what it is," she said, both sounding and looking quite terse.

Shrugging, Ethan popped the small square into his mouth and chewed. This ranked as one the best he'd tasted. As he swallowed, he reached for his notebook and jotted down some impressions, as he had done with each previous piece he'd tasted. Oatmeal wheat should stay the same. . .maybe a few revisions—it could probably be more moist. *Mostly needs a name change,* he scribbled.

As he finished, he could sense Dana leaning ever so slightly toward him—and his notebook. Ethan hated the feeling of having someone watch him so closely. He shut the book, and Dana eased back, looking quite uninterested.

Ethan held back a grin, realizing that Dana seemed terribly interested in what he wrote. Ethan supposed he could share his observations, but quite honestly, he didn't feel comfortable doing so. There would be no way to guess how she might react. He'd hoped to get started on better footing with her this morning, but she'd spilled coffee all over her hand and gotten upset with him when he'd tried to help. After that, in the break room, she snubbed him in front of everyone present—all but ignored him, as though he didn't exist.

Since then, she had stayed as silent as a stone—only talking when he asked her a direct question. She was extremely knowledgeable about all aspects of the company, and he understood why the Gradys chose her to help him. If they had picked anyone else, his time would have been wasted, as he probably still would have ended up asking Dana everything he needed to know.

She had a great head for business—exactly the type of person he would choose to run the administrative side of his restaurant if he ever got around to opening one, rather than simply helping other people fix theirs. Correction, he decided. He'd like to work with her if he could get some assurances that she was actually a real person instead of some sort of robot who had no idea of how to interact with other people.

Ethan looked at his watch. "It's a little after noon," he announced to Dana. She nodded in agreement but didn't reply.

Ethan closed his eyes briefly. *Lord, help me through this. I can't imagine spending the next few months or even hours with this woman if she's going to act like this the entire time.*

"How about lunch?" he suggested.

Dana opened her mouth and closed it. From the look on her face, she almost seemed unsure of whether there would be any benefit to getting away from work if she still had to be in his company. Ethan supposed if they went their own separate ways for lunch, she would probably be much happier. The idea of suggesting they do just that crossed his mind, but Ethan decided against it. Although his plan to get to know his assistant had not failed, it had been subject to numerous delays. Even though she seemed bent on making his workday miserable, he didn't yet want to throw in the towel.

"How can you be hungry? You've been eating bread all morning."

He shrugged. "I need to clear my palate before I can finish the rest of these samples, so I want to eat something besides bread for lunch."

"Oh, the trials of being a chef," Dana said, not sounding at all sympathetic.

Without waiting for her to agree with him, Ethan stood up, retrieved his coat from the chair, and waited for her to do the same. "We'll have to take your car, of course, so you can pick the place."

Dana actually smiled. "Sure, I think that can be arranged. And I'm feeling generous, so I'll treat."

The sentence sounded like an oxymoron. The words "Dana" and "generous" didn't seem to go together. Ethan supposed he should feel wary of her sudden cooperation, but he felt too hungry to give it much thought. Besides, maybe she just needed awhile to warm up to him.

As he followed her to the car, he wondered where they would be dining. His mouth watered at the thought of a big, juicy hamburger and thick, homemade French fries, and he hoped she would pick a place that served a good burger. But he couldn't very well offer to let Dana pick the place, then change his mind—especially since she had offered to pay.

*Oh well,* he decided. The least he could do was be gracious, since she seemed to be making an effort to be nice.

Dana drove a short distance and pulled into a parking lot of a small diner. The place didn't look fancy by a long shot. Instead, it reflected years of wear and tear. Although some people he knew would do their best to stay away from eateries like this, Ethan didn't mind. He'd learned a long time ago that some of the less-elaborate establishments had some of the best food. Besides, the parking lot was full, and a steady stream of people came and went. That had to count for something.

Dana pulled into a parking space but didn't make a move to get out of the car.

Ethan cleared his throat. "So, is this the place?" He tried not to sound overly enthusiastic, not knowing if Dana would think he might be trying too hard to be friendly.

At first, she didn't seem to have heard him, but just as he opened his mouth to speak up again, she glanced over at him with a strange look on her face. She shook her head. "No. . .I took a wrong turn. I pulled in here to turn around." Dana shifted the car in reverse and quickly pulled out of the parking lot.

Ethan felt more than a little disappointed. The smells coming from that place were wonderful, and he hated to leave it behind. Apparently, the diner didn't suit Dana's style. He'd have to remember how to get here on his own sometime.

Finally, after several more minutes of driving, they arrived at a small, quiet café.

Ethan felt like groaning. No way was he going to find his hamburger here.

The heartiest thing he found on the menu was a chicken salad. Although it turned out to be rather tasty, the salad wasn't as filling as he had hoped it would be.

Ethan tried not to let his disappointment over Dana's choice of a restaurant show for two reasons. At first, he'd thought she really wanted to be on friendly terms with him. Although moments of quiet did settle over them, the tone was different. The silence Ethan endured all morning had been stony, but now it had become amicable. Second, Dana seemed really anxious of his opinion of the place. For some reason, whether or not he liked this place seemed very important to her. He could tell by the hopeful look on her face, and though he probably wouldn't want to dine here every day, he'd enjoyed it well enough.

When the check came, Ethan offered to go half and half with Dana. Places like this were not exactly inexpensive, and he didn't want her to feel financially pressured on his account. Dana firmly, but kindly, refused his help. At least, at first she did. She tried to write a check, but the waiter informed her that they did not accept checks.

"But I don't have any cash with me."

The waiter shook his head. "Perhaps a credit card?"

Dana nodded and began searching through her purse. Less than a minute later, she came up empty handed. "I'm sorry, but I don't have my credit card with me. I usually leave it at home unless I know I'm going to be using it for something specific. Couldn't I just write a check just this once?"

The waiter lifted his eyebrows. "Madam, we accept cash or credit."

A look of sheer mortification washed over Dana's face. Other customers were beginning to glance in their direction.

Ethan pulled out his wallet and handed over his credit card. "My treat this time," he told Dana. He hated to sound as though he were taking over like a rescuing knight, but really there had been no other choice.

Apparently, Dana agreed. "Thank you," she whispered as the waiter carried away his card to process the receipt. "I'm so sorry about this. I'm just so embarrassed. I should have realized this place didn't take checks."

Ethan frowned. "I thought you came here often."

Dana sighed. "Not really. I actually prefer much simpler fare, but I worried that you might want something fancier, since you're the famous chef and all." She leaned closer and lowered her voice a notch. "Remember that diner we went to at first? I actually wanted to take you there just to spite you. I figured Mr. 'I need to clear my palate' wouldn't enjoy that place."

Ethan leaned back and laughed, not caring if others were watching. "So how'd we end up here?"

Dana looked down at the table. "My conscience got me at the last second," she admitted. "I drove away as fast as I could and didn't look back. I repented all the way here."

Ethan laughed again, then leaned closer toward her. "I'll let you in on a little secret of my own. I could have cried when we left that diner. The smells in the parking lot were fantastic."

Dana's eyes widened. "You mean, you wouldn't have minded eating lunch there?"

"No, and I insist we go there next time."

Dana looked relieved. "Good. And I'll treat. They do take checks there."

The two of them shared a laugh before Ethan decided to broach a more sensitive topic. "Dana," he began, "I have no idea why things have been strained between us, but I want us to be friends. If you can't commit to that, I'd like for us to at least be civil. I think that will be an important part of the probability of us succeeding at this job."

She nodded slowly. "I agree. I haven't been all that fun to be around, and I'm sorry. Will you forgive me?"

Ethan nodded. "Sure. Would it be too tacky of me to ask why you've been upset with me?"

A startled look passed over Dana's face, and Ethan hurried to clarify his question. "I'm not trying to prod where I shouldn't. My only concern is that I've done something to offend you, and I don't want to do it again."

"I see. . . ."

Before she could answer, a woman walked up to their table.

"Excuse me," she said cautiously. "I hate to interrupt, but aren't you Ethan Miles, the chef?"

Ethan nodded, and the woman smiled. "Oh, I love your cookbook," she said. "In fact, I wish I had it with me so you could autograph it. Remember the dinner party recipes you had when you were featured in *The Household Chef's Magazine?* I have to tell you, they turned out fabulously. I made them for a garden party last summer, and everyone just raved."

"Well, thank you," Ethan said. "I'm always glad to hear that someone enjoys my recipes."

"Oh, of course," said the woman. "I'm hoping that you'll have a cooking show again sometime soon. Why did the network cancel it?"

"Well, actually, my contract ended, and I didn't feel ready to renew," Ethan explained. "I liked doing the show, but it took away from my regular schedule. Right now, I'm doing freelance work for independent restaurants and bakeries in addition to writing my next cookbook. Maybe later I'll be able to juggle all that with a cooking show again."

"I certainly hope so," the woman agreed. "But in the meantime, I'll be looking forward to your next cookbook. When can I find it in stores?"

"I'm still writing it, but it should be on the shelves around this time next year. Next February at the latest."

"Perfect," the woman said. "I don't want to take all of your time, but thanks for chatting with me."

"And thank you for your comments about my cookbook."

As soon as the woman left, the waiter returned with the receipt. "I guess we should get back to the office," Ethan told Dana. "We've got a plate of bread just waiting to be tasted."

In all honesty, he wanted to finish their previous conversation, but he wasn't sure if this would be a good time for the question he'd been on the verge of asking. The last thing he wanted to do was cause Dana to feel pressured. Maybe in a few days the topic would come up again.

❧

"What a day," Dana sighed, as she unlocked the door to her house. Ethan had handled the situation at lunch graciously, and although she still had her doubts about whether his influence would be good for the bakeries, she had gained more respect for him.

She still felt remorse for giving him the silent treatment that morning, and she hated to think of what her mother would say if she heard how Dana had behaved.

*I'm acting like a spoiled little kid.* Dana shook her head. "This has to stop," she said firmly. "Tomorrow, I'm going to go in and do my job. If his influence will hurt the company, I'll trust the Lord to fix whatever goes wrong."

The aspect of leaving all of her uncertainties to prayer lifted a weight from Dana's shoulders. With a smile, she headed to the kitchen to fix dinner.

❧

"What do you think of adding cranberries to the raisin bread?" Ethan asked.

"Well," Dana paused and put her hand over her mouth to mask a yawn. "I don't know. You're the chef, right?"

Ethan shrugged. "But you're my assistant. You know the market; you know the customers." He stirred a few spoonfuls of yeast into a bowl of warm water and set it aside. "Tell me how you think it will taste."

Dana opened her mouth, only to let another yawn escape. Mortified, she apologized as she continued to fiddle with the apron strings she still struggled to fasten behind her back. When had she ever worn an apron? At any rate, the women on old sitcoms from the fifties made tying an apron look so easy. Then again, they'd worn decorative, frilly little aprons, while she stood, draped in a huge white cloth that could have doubled as a small bed sheet.

"Let me help you with that." Ethan crossed the room. "You don't have to tie it behind your back. Wrap it around and bring it back to the front, then tie it."

Dana nodded and did as Ethan instructed. Of course, he got to wear a chef's jacket, not an apron. When she finished, she caught a glimpse of her reflection in one of the windows. "This thing is not exactly figure flattering," she murmured.

Taking a seat on a barstool, Dana yawned again. "Tell me again why we're here at five-thirty in the morning."

"We need to use a fully equipped kitchen to test the recipes. If we come any later, we'll be in the way of the bakers who work here, so we had to come early."

Dana nodded. "So why didn't we use the kitchen at the main office so we could come in to work during normal hours?"

"Mr. Grady said the floors and countertops are being re-done. The contractors wanted to start right away, or else they would take another job. So we're stuck here with early hours until that kitchen gets done."

Mr. Grady had been trying to schedule that remodel for a few months now, and it was just Dana's luck as a definite allergic-to-morning person that the work would have to begin at this hour. Most days she counted herself fortunate to be alert by nine. Anything before that seemed to be a blur. "Okay, what do I need to do?"

"Take notes for now," he said. "I need help, but I'm picky about measuring everything myself when I'm creating."

Dana didn't argue. Taking notes suited her just fine. At least, it would *after* she made her coffee. "Can I interest you in coffee?"

Ethan, engrossed in examining the current raisin bread recipe, nodded absent-mindedly.

Dana powered up the small, kitchen coffee maker and located some coffee beans. This wouldn't be as good as the stuff they made in the huge commercial machines for the customers, but at this early hour, she couldn't be picky. While the drink brewed, she returned to her chair, notebook in hand.

"Ginger!" Ethan said.

"Excuse me?"

Ethan gestured toward the notebook. "Write that down. Ginger. I need ginger in this bread."

"Okay," Dana said, making a note of it. "Anything else?"

"Not yet. . .but keep your ears open. If I say something, just jot it down. It'll help for later reference."

Dana had a feeling this might turn out to be a long baking session. She was used to spending hours in the kitchen making holiday meals with her family, but she'd never put in that many kitchen hours at work.

While measuring cups of flour into a bowl, Ethan glanced at Dana. "You feeling okay?" He looked concerned.

"I don't look okay?" Dana asked, only half joking. She smiled and waved his concerns away. "You must be more of a morning person than I am."

Before he could answer, the timer on the machine went off, signaling the coffee had finished percolating. "Stay there. I'll get it," Ethan said. In moments, he had poured two mugs and set them on the counter. Taking a seat next to her, he took a long sip. "This is good coffee."

Dana took a drink and murmured her agreement. After another sip, she said, "I'm ready to work now."

Ethan shook his head. "Let's finish our coffee." After a short pause, he added, "Maybe we can talk—you know, have a conversation."

Laughing, Dana ignored the uncertain look in his eyes. "I see where you're going, and I'll just apologize for yesterday again. I was in a silly mood that I don't really want to talk about. However," she took another drink, "it won't happen again."

Ethan looked relieved. "I'm glad. Now we can get to know each other." His smile was warm and genuine.

Dana felt at ease. She could get used to this. Sitting in a kitchen while a handsome chef baked bread. . .

*Oh, quit it. Just yesterday you couldn't stand the sight of the man; now you're practically swooning.* Before her thoughts could wander any further, she spoke up. "So tell me about you."

He took a deep breath. "I'll give you the condensed version, since we have to get to work today." He set his mug down, a thoughtful look on his face. "Well, I'm twenty-nine years old. I'm originally from Chicago, and I wanted to be a fireman since I was five years old." He stopped and looked at Dana. "Are you sure you really want to hear all this?"

She nodded. "Yes. So how did you end up as a chef?"

"When I was in the tenth grade, my class took a tour of a fancy restaurant. We got to watch the chefs make crème brulee and bananas foster." He laughed. "That hooked me. I'd never seen a dessert you had to set on fire, and from then on I was convinced that I too was called to set perfectly good desserts on fire instead of dousing burning buildings.

"I went to a culinary institute in New York and graduated with honors. I've written two cookbooks, worked at famous restaurants, had a cooking show, and now I do independent consulting."

"Wow," said Dana. "I think I've seen your cooking show once or twice. I knew you looked familiar, but I couldn't put the pieces together until that lady at the café mentioned it yesterday." She quirked an eyebrow. "I just hope the Gradys can handle the bill for your services."

He laughed. "I'm doing this job at a cut rate. I'm not charging half of what this is worth."

"Why?" Dana asked, curious.

"I like to help people, and I'm scouting the country, looking for the ideal place to open my own establishment. This is a good way to travel, get a handle on regional restaurants, and keep from digging into my savings to pay for it."

Dana blinked. He certainly exuded confidence. Yesterday, she might have rankled at this statement and thought him rather conceited. In all honesty, she did her best to remain positive even now, as he spoke.

It somehow bothered her that he referred to the Gradys as an almost charity case. One half of what his services were worth, her foot! Hadn't Mr. Grady said Ethan's bill was rather sizable? If this were a discount, she'd hate to see the regular price.

Ethan gave her an odd look. "Did I say something wrong?"

Dana sighed. He seemed sincere enough. Maybe he was one of those people who couldn't help boasting every now and then. He'd probably meant no harm. Besides, in all honesty, she knew nothing of what this type of consultation would be worth. She merely worked for a restaurateur and still had a lot to learn about the business.

She smiled and assured Ethan she was all right. "So what have you enjoyed the most about your job?"

He didn't answer right away. "I don't know. Every day has so many little rewards. If I had to pick just one thing. . .I'd say. . . designing and baking my sister's wedding cake." He shrugged. "I know it sounds silly, but it actually gave me a chance to feel like I was a part of the whole thing. My dad paid for the wedding, my mom and sister planned it, so the cake was my humble contribution."

"That's so sweet," Dana said, impressed. "Now that I know a good baker, I'll have to put your name down in my wedding planning book."

Ethan blinked, a surprised look on his face. "Oh. I didn't

know you were engaged."

Dana watched his gaze travel to the bare ring finger on her left hand. "Congratulations," he said, his voice sounding flat. He picked up his coffee mug and headed back to the bowl where he'd been mixing bread.

Dana, understanding his assumption, laughed, feeling a tad sheepish. "Well, thanks, but I guess I have to admit that congratulations aren't in order yet. I'm not engaged."

He looked up from the mixture he stirred. "Oh? Just waiting for him to pop the question, huh?"

Dana cleared her throat and set her mug on the countertop. "Actually, I'm not seeing anyone. I just like to keep notes for wedding ideas so when the right guy comes along. . ." she trailed off, feeling embarrassed. Why had she told him all of this?

Dana decided to try again. "My sister-in-law is a wedding coordinator, and she always tells people that if they have more than a general idea of what they want for the big day, it will make things easier when it's time to sit down and plan."

Although he seemed to be holding back a smile, he replied, "She's right. I've seen people dissolve into tears just trying to pick a cake. If you're not careful, planning a wedding can be stressful."

"So I guess I'm on the right track," she said, ready to put the topic behind them. Talking to a complete stranger about her wedding dreams made her a little uneasy. "What about you? Are you married, engaged, anything like that?" As soon as the last sentence left her mouth, Dana cringed inside. *Anything like that? What was that supposed to mean?*

Unfortunately, Ethan hadn't missed her awkward question and decided to answer it. "No to married. No to engaged." A thoughtful look came over his face. "I don't understand the last question. 'Anything like that?' If you explain it, maybe I can come up with an answer."

Dana chuckled. "Okay, okay, it was a silly question. It just means, what about you? Are you attached?" She could feel her face burning as she asked the question.

He stopped stirring and let the spoon rest on the side of the bowl. "Does someone want to know?"

Dana tried not to lose her composure. "No one I know," she informed him in a matter-of-fact tone.

He nodded and resumed stirring. "Tell 'No One' that I'm as single as can be."

Dana couldn't think of a word to say. This was not good. Now he probably thought she had a more than friendly interest in him. Not good at all. She changed the subject. "I guess I should tell you all about me now," she suggested.

Ethan shook his head. "Nope. We've got work to do."

Relieved, Dana reached for her notebook. Work, she could do. It was constructive and would keep her from thinking about Ethan's expressive brown eyes. She returned to her seat and stared at her paper.

"Why don't you tell me all about you this evening? Over dinner?"

Dana looked up at him, and their eyes met. He waited for a response, but she couldn't decide. "Dinner?" she repeated.

"Yes. Remember, I'm also visiting restaurants when I'm not working. That's my own project, research for my eventual restaurant. I hoped you could suggest a good place."

"Oh," Dana said. He wasn't asking her out on a date. Her emotions were a mixture of relief and disappointment. He just wanted her to pick the restaurant. "I guess that would be okay," she said slowly.

"Good. And don't pick that café we went to again," he said, not looking up from the spices he measured.

Dana simply nodded. This was doable. It was nothing out

of the ordinary. She would go on a business outing with a chef tonight. Not a date. This was business related. And that was acceptable. Right?

*Sure, it's fine*, she reassured herself. *So why do I feel butter-flies in my stomach? Only because he's a single, handsome, slightly egotistical chef who I have to work with for the next few months, that's why,* she scolded herself.

"Anise," said Ethan. "Write that down, Dana."

Dana wrote the word "anise" three times, thinking about how special her name sounded when Ethan said it.

## six

"It's your turn now," Ethan said after he and Dana ordered their meals. She gave him a puzzled look.

"My turn for what?"

"To tell me about yourself," he reminded her. He took a drink of water and waited.

Dana smiled. "Right, it's my turn. Unfortunately, there's not all that much to tell."

"I'd still like to hear it."

"Okay," she said. "I'm the youngest of eight kids. Otis, Latrice, Jackson, Max, Albert, Anthony, Sheryl, then me." She laughed. "Believe me, we never had a dull moment at our house."

"Seven brothers and sisters?" This surprised him. Dana seemed so serious and almost old for her age, unlike other people he'd met who were the youngest in their families. He couldn't imagine having that many siblings, especially ones older than himself. "Wow, how did it feel to be the youngest?"

Dana grinned and, without hesitation, replied, "Like I had nine parents instead of two."

Ethan laughed. "Sounds like your brothers and sisters took their jobs seriously."

Dana shook her head. "I don't think they were always that enthralled with the job. I was the little one, so after the initial newness wore off, they realized they were stuck with me."

"So they tried to dodge you?"

Dana shrugged. "Sometimes. It just depended on what kind of mood they were in. I'll admit I got my share of babying—

especially from my brother, Max. Even when the rest of them got sick of me, he generally took up for me. He's still the most tenderhearted of the bunch."

"Really? What's the age difference between you two?"

"Eight years. When he went to Kansas City for college, it broke my heart. I was only ten, so I thought he might be mad at me and left me behind on purpose."

The waitress arrived with their food and interrupted the conversation for a moment. After they began eating, Ethan picked up where they had left off. "Are you and your brother still close?"

Dana tilted her head to the side. "Not as much, I guess. He got married last year. He and Stacy will celebrate their first anniversary in a few weeks."

Ethan nodded. "Any nieces, nephews?"

Dana nodded. "Lots. I'd bore you if I started telling all of my 'Aunt Dana' stories. The oldest, Otis Jr., will be going away to college in the fall, and the youngest won't be here until June."

"Boy or girl?"

Dana shrugged. "Max and Stacy don't want to know, so it'll be a surprise. They told us at Christmas, and they're so excited."

"Sounds like you're a busy aunt."

Dana laughed. "Yes, only three of us are still single—me and the twins, Albert and Anthony. That means we are the ones the rest of them can count on for free babysitting. And my house is the destination of choice for impromptu sleepovers." She grinned, her eyes sparkling. "Word has gotten around with my nieces that I have a pretty nice makeup collection, and I don't mind letting little fingers play with my lipstick. It's also known that I like to spend some time at the Galleria on the weekends."

"The Galleria. . .So you're a fan of shopping malls, huh?"

"You bet," said Dana.

"I guess there's no contest between spending the night at your house or with your two brothers?"

She shook her head. "Only for the girls. Albert and Anthony have a major collection of video games, and they will invent something to do before they step foot in a mall, so the boys gravitate toward their house."

"Hey, I like video games, myself," Ethan said. "Where do they live?"

Dana sighed impatiently. "Oh, please, not you too. My dad teases that the only reason they're still single is because they would have too much difficulty dividing up all of their games if one of them got married."

Ethan laughed outright. "I have to confess, whenever I travel, I usually pack my system and a few games in my suitcase. It helps me to relax, gives me something to do besides think about work."

Dana shook her head and laughed. "They have the opposite effect on me. I concentrate too much on trying to work all of the buttons, and I never have fun since the other person always wins."

Ethan nodded. "My sister does that. I'll have to teach you how to play and enjoy yourself at the same time. Besides, it's not about winning. It's just for fun."

Dana gave him a wry smile. "Tell that to Albert and Anthony."

After they finished, the waitress reappeared, wondering if they'd like to order dessert. Dana decided to pass, but Ethan wanted to taste their flourless chocolate cake, so she decided she would have coffee while he had dessert. Ethan ordered and asked for two forks.

"Sure you don't want a bite before I start eating this?" Ethan asked before he tasted it.

Dana shrugged. "Okay, maybe a bite." She reached for the extra fork and took a tiny piece. "It's delicious," she admitted.

"Sure you don't want to share it?"

"I'm sure. But thanks for offering."

Later, as they walked to his car, the January wind whipped around them, blowing Dana's scarf to the ground. Ethan bent down to retrieve it.

His fingers brushed hers as he handed the scarf to her. Dana's hands were little and cold to the touch. "Shouldn't you be wearing gloves in this weather?"

Dana blinked. "I must have left them at home."

Ethan reached into his pocket and handed her his own gloves. "Then wear mine. It'll take the car a little while to warm up."

"Thank you," Dana said quietly. The smile she gave him made up for the fact that his own hands were freezing.

"I feel bad taking these from you," she said, lifting up her hands, now engulfed in his gloves. They were so baggy on her tiny hands that Ethan wondered if they would do any good.

"Are you sure you don't need them? You're the one who has to touch the steering wheel, and I know how much I hate driving without gloves."

"I'll be fine. But if you insist on helping me, I do need to ask a favor." He opened the passenger's side door for Dana. After she got inside, he hurried over to his own side and got in.

The steering wheel felt brutally cold, as Dana had predicted, but Ethan tried not to show it. He gripped the wheel as if it might even be warm. As he maneuvered the car out of the parking lot, Dana reminded him of his earlier question.

"So, what's the favor?"

He hesitated. He'd been trying to work up the nerve to ask this for the past few days at work but hadn't decided if his request might be too intrusive. Maybe he had spoken too soon and should wait until later. The last thing he wanted to do was ruin the friendship he and Dana seemed to have forged over the past day.

He shook his head. "Never mind."

Out of the corner of his eye, he saw Dana purse her lips together and tilt her head to the side. He tried to change the subject.

"What about sports?" he asked. "I hear a lot about the Blues. Maybe we should take in a game sometime. You know, so I can get the full St. Louis experience."

Dana laughed. "Sure. I'm not a big hockey fan, but we can go to see the Blues. And if you're still here when baseball season rolls around, we can go see a Cardinals game."

"Anything else I'm missing that I need to experience as a temporary St. Louisan?" he asked, smiling.

"Lots," Dana told him. "Since you're into tasting the area cuisine, you'll have to visit Ted Drewes's; but you'll have to wait a little while because they're only open February through December, so in a couple of weeks, I'll take you there. You should see all of the people lined up outside in the summertime, waiting to order frozen custard."

Ethan grinned. "I'll make it a point not to leave until I've had some."

"But you didn't trick me, Mr. Ethan D. Miles," she teased. "You're changing the subject. Now about that favor. . ."

Ethan sighed. He hadn't gotten off the hook with that one. He should have kept his mouth shut. "All right, if you must know," he began.

Dana nodded, waiting for him to continue.

"I hate to ask you this because I don't want you to feel like I'm pushing my way into your weekend, but I know you're a Christian, and I need a place to go to church while I'm here. I already missed going this past Sunday, and I thought I'd see if you would allow me to attend your church."

Dana was quiet for a moment, then burst into laughter.

"What's so funny?"

When Dana finally stopped, she answered, "As if I could keep someone out of a church. Churches don't belong to people, Ethan, they belong to God."

"I know that," he said. "Still, I wondered if you would dread working with me all week, then have to see me on Sundays. Saturday would be the only day you could escape me."

"Me?" Dana asked in an overly innocent voice. "Why would I want to escape you?"

This time it was Ethan's turn to laugh. "You're kidding me, right? Let me refresh your memory. Remember last Friday night when we met at dinner? And Monday morning when you treated me like I had the plague in front of everyone at the office? How about the lunch date when you tried to take me somewhere I'd hate on purpose? For what reason? I don't know, since you refused to tell—"

"Okay, okay." She laughed. "I get the picture, and I apologize again. But, no, I won't be upset if you come to my church. I go to the same church as the Gradys anyway. . . ," she trailed off, midsentence. "Wait a minute. Didn't you think of asking them where they went to church?"

Ethan shrugged. He realized that not much escaped Dana's notice. "I guess I could have asked them," he began. "But maybe I decided I'd rather attend the place where my charming assistant goes."

A long moment of silence settled over them before Dana finally answered, her voice flat. "Oh, I see. The charming assistant. I hope you're not expecting me to take notes about ingredients during the sermon."

Ethan glanced over at her. She stopped smiling, turned away from him, and stared out of the window. They were now rounding the corner to her block, and Ethan struggled to find the right words to say. Knowing Dana, she would hop out of the car, leaving him feeling awkward and in the dark about what he'd said to upset her.

Not knowing how to proceed with the conversation, Ethan opened his mouth and started talking. "About church on Sunday," he said. Dana didn't respond, but he continued, grasping at straws. "Since I really don't know my way around that well—I mean, I know how to get to my apartment, work, the grocery store, and now your house. But would you mind if I. . ." he paused, slowing to a stop in front of her house.

Sighing deeply, Dana nodded. "That's fine. You can meet me here and follow me."

Ethan had a feeling he might be treading on thin ice, but he spoke up anyway. "I was hoping we could ride together. I'd be willing to drive."

"Well, I'd prefer to drive myself—"

"Then I'll ride with you," he finished. "But I'll chip in money for gas."

Dana sighed again. "Fine." She opened the door a crack, then turned to face him. "Thank you for dinner." The stoic look in her eyes melted away for a moment. "I. . .I had a good time."

"So did I. Thanks for coming."

"Thank you for asking me." She gave him the tiniest of smiles and hurried out of the car.

Ethan watched her make her way to her front door and waited until he determined that she got safely inside before pulling away from the curb.

As he thought back over the events of their evening, he smiled. He'd had a good time, even if it hadn't been an official date. Dana could call it whatever she wanted, but it was as good as a date, in his opinion. And now, he'd managed to arrange to ride to church with her Sunday. He might even be able to take her to dinner afterwards.

ॐ

Dana closed the front door with a sigh. What had happened here? If Ethan didn't feel the need to remind her that she was nothing more than the *assistant*, she might be able to have a few hours of uninterrupted fun with him. He was humorous, he was charming, he was good looking. . .he was a Christian. He was perfect. Maybe.

But why did he constantly have to assert himself as The Boss? Wasn't this evening supposed to be a nonwork event? Even he had called it a date during their conversation at dinner.

Dana trudged up the stairs to her bedroom without bothering to take off her coat. She put on her pajamas and applied a beauty mask. The label claimed the mask would do an amazing number of miracles, including cleanse her pores and help her to relax.

Shrugging, Dana turned off the overhead light and flipped on one of the floor lamps because it gave off a soft, dim glow. As she sat in her overstuffed armchair, she leaned back with her eyes closed, waiting for the mask to do its work. While she rested, she became increasingly aware of a familiar scent—the scent of Ethan's cologne, to be exact.

Somewhat startled, she sat up straighter, trying to determine if her imagination had grown a tad overactive. As she looked around the room, she saw no clue that explained the woodsy fragrance. After a few minutes, Dana decided that she had probably been thinking about Ethan a little too much. After all, hadn't she just seen on the news the results of a research project that explained how people were likely to link certain smells and foods to memories? That explained it. Thinking about Ethan made her imagine his cologne.

Dana chuckled, wondering if anyone would ever be able to

invent a way to imagine something like chocolate or ice cream and be able to taste it without actually ingesting any.

Closing her eyes, she leaned back in her chair again, but this time her rumpled coat, which she had tossed over the back of the chair, made it hard for her to relax.

Dana swiftly tossed the coat clear across the room, aiming for her bed. She'd learned this trick from watching Albert and Anthony clean their rooms in a hurry. Living with so many brothers had its drawbacks, but she'd definitely picked up some interesting housecleaning tips from them. At least she didn't just throw clothes into her closet the way they did. She still utilized hangers, whereas they liked to toss shoes and other items inside and quickly shut the door.

Before she could close her eyes again, Dana noticed something on the floor. Two large black objects lay on the other side of the room, near the foot of the bed. With a shriek, she jumped up in the chair, too scared to turn toward them again. Whatever they were, they hadn't been there a few minutes ago. In the dim room, they looked particularly ominous, and she wished she had left the ceiling light on instead of the floor lamp.

Forcing herself to take deep breaths, she tried to remain calm. The first thing she needed to do was determine what those *things* were, then get out of the room and call one of her brothers to come over and remove them.

Frowning, Dana wondered if this might be another one of Anthony or Albert's jokes. They lived a five-minute drive away and had a key to her house for emergencies. They knew she hated critters of any kind, even ants or ladybugs, and she kept her house exceptionally clean to discourage any little visitors from taking up residence.

Her brothers, on the other hand, had collected bugs, worms, and pets, causing her no small amount of distress during her girlhood years. Sliding a frog or hamster into her bed had been a great source of entertainment—and ultimately punishment—for those two.

She remembered once asking her mother why Albert and Anthony had to be *twins*, instead of just *one* boy. To her six-year-old reasoning, contending with only one of them would have been much easier.

Dana hopped down from her chair, swooped up the cordless phone from the table a few feet from the chair, and jumped back to her perch, still safe from her intruders.

She hit a button on her speed dial and listened to the phone ring several times. Apparently, her brothers were trying to pretend they weren't even at home!

While she stood on the chair, waiting for someone to pick up the phone, Dana had a horrifying thought. What if those things crept off while she talked on the phone, making a plea for help?

A vision of sliding her feet into an expensive pair of shoes, her toes meeting a dead—or even worse—a live critter made Dana grimace. That did it. She would stay in the room while she waited for backup. If those things wandered somewhere, she'd at least have a good idea of where they went.

Before she could give the idea more thought, Anthony answered the phone. "Hello?" he said, sounding somewhat groggy.

Dana's teased-little-sister instincts kicked in. She could imagine the two of them sitting on their couch, just waiting for her to call, and eventually answering the phone, pretending they had been asleep in order to prolong the joke.

"Oh, please," she replied, her voice dripping with sarcasm. "I know you are not *even* asleep. Get over here and get these things out. Now!"

Anthony sounded more awake, "What?"

"You heard me," Dana said, her voice alternating between

quavering and yelling. "I want you two to get over here and get these things out of here. It's not funny!"

In the background, she could hear Albert asking what was going on. Anthony explained, still pretending he didn't know what she was talking about. She sighed heavily.

"What things?" Albert asked, taking the phone from Anthony.

Dana's temper flared. She could be in danger, and they were taking this too far. "You know good and well what they are. Those. . .black things! The ones you put in my bedroom. Come get them now, or I'm calling Mom and Dad!" Before they could say another word, she clicked the phone off. The twins would have to go some great lengths to make peace with her after this. She should be in bed, getting her rest. As it stood now, she would have a hard time falling asleep, wondering if they had accidentally forgotten some of their other creatures.

Remembering her resolve to watch the creatures to make sure they didn't escape, Dana slowly turned around and took a quick look. A sigh of relief escaped from her lips. They were still there, in the exact same position.

*Weird. Why haven't those things moved?* She twisted a bit to get a better view. They were still there. And now they didn't look like things at all. They looked like. . .

"Oh, no," Dana groaned. She got down from her chair, feeling like an absolute ninny. They weren't live critters; they were Ethan's gloves, and they must have fallen out of her coat pockets when she tossed it across the room. They also accounted for the smell of Ethan's cologne.

The screech of tires interrupted her thoughts. She heard car doors open but didn't hear them slam shut. Albert and Anthony. How in the world would she explain this to them? Next, she heard the front door creaking open, then loud footsteps rumbling up the stairs.

Seconds later, her brothers entered the room, both wearing pajamas, one holding a baseball bat and the other wielding a golf club. The intense expressions on their faces made Dana burst into laughter.

"Where is it?" Albert shouted, his voice full of worry. Dana felt instant remorse. She'd gotten them out of bed, yelled at them, and scared the daylights out of them, all for a pair of gloves. She seriously doubted they would find her explanation amusing, but she tried anyway.

After several moments, they lowered their impromptu weapons. Albert, the more easygoing of the pair, reached out for the gloves. "So you went on a date with this guy, he loaned you his gloves, they ended up on the floor, and you thought we had played some kind of trick on you."

"You *mistakenly* thought," Anthony supplied in a mock fatherly voice.

"Yes. I'm really sorry for getting you out of bed. It's been a long night, so why don't you go home, and we can all go to bed?"

Anthony grinned. "No way. This is too good. Tell us more."

"More? Why?"

Albert shrugged. "Because we want to hear more. It isn't every day our sister has a date."

Dana put her hands on her hips. "This is none of your business. So go home. Now." She made a shooing motion to emphasize her point.

Anthony shrugged. "You know, we could argue that you owe us—that maybe you even set us up, having us rush over here, with just enough time to throw on boots and grab our keys. Maybe you didn't have a date. Maybe you put that stuff on your face and tried to scare us, looking like some kind of alien."

Dana touched a finger to her cheek and stared at the

greenish-brown residue on her finger. She'd forgotten all about the mask. "Ha, ha, laugh all you want. It was an honest mistake, and you know I don't play practical jokes."

"These are a man's gloves," Albert said to Anthony, as if that proved her point.

Anthony grabbed the gloves away from his brother and sniffed them. "Yeah, and they're covered in cologne. Where does this guy work? The cologne factory?" Anthony wrinkled his nose and held the gloves away in an exaggerated fashion.

Dana shrugged apologetically. "Look, you guys, I'm sorry to put you out, but I'm too tired to talk right now. Maybe tomorrow or Sunday."

"So when do we get to meet him?" Anthony asked.

"Never," Dana said in frustration.

Her brothers exchanged knowing glances.

"What?" Dana wanted to know.

"What's this guy like?" asked Albert.

"He's a nice guy," Dana said, not wanting to have them conduct a brotherly evaluation of Ethan, especially since he'd made it clear they had a working relationship and nothing more.

"Nice, huh?" said Albert.

"And it's over between you two?" added Anthony.

"Yes," she answered.

"So why'd you go out with him in the first place?" Anthony asked.

"Because. . ." was all she could say. What else could she say without embarrassing herself? *He's ideal husband material, and I like him, but he doesn't like me?*

No, she didn't want to put that on her brothers' shoulders right now. Pests that they were, they would still be a little upset with any guy who they thought wasn't treating her well.

"Because what?" Albert pressed.

Dana groaned. Why couldn't they drop this already? "Because. . .I don't know. Nothing clicked, okay?"

"But he's nice." Anthony stated. He and Albert exchanged that look again.

"Yes, yes, yes, he's nice. So go home now, okay?"

Her brothers obediently turned and headed back down the stairs. Dana followed and locked the door behind them. Through the window, she could see their car, parked at a crazy angle, the doors wide open. They would have a cold ride home. Even with all of their pestering, Dana was grateful that they lived nearby and were willing to come to her rescue. A close-knit family provided such comfort in so many ways. Still, she longed to have her own family like so many of her other siblings now had.

Dana trudged back upstairs and began the process of washing the now-crusted mask off of her face. Hopefully her brothers would just let the memory of this escapade fall by the wayside.

No, this one would probably go in the history books as far as Anthony and Albert were concerned. She only had herself to blame. If she hadn't been in such a daydreaming mood after getting home, she would have realized the mysterious things were just gloves long before making the phone call to her brothers.

After settling in under her warm comforter, Dana's last thoughts were about her dinner with Ethan. Too bad she had gotten her hopes so high about Ethan, but he wanted a business relationship with nothing more than friendship. She could deal with that. Hopefully.

## seven

Dana didn't even see the ice. She *did* see her foot, enclosed in a sensible black pump, flying up in the air as the rest of her landed on the ground.

Next, she saw Ethan leaning over her. "Wow! Are you okay?"

"My pride is going to sting for awhile." She took hold of Ethan's extended hand and regained her footing. *Thank goodness I wore the long wool skirt this morning.*

"Are you hurt?" Ethan asked.

Dana took a tentative step forward, relieved that she had miraculously escaped a sprain or, even worse, a broken bone.

"I'm okay," she assured him. Her cheeks burned as she felt the curious stares of her fellow church members. She would have preferred to enter the church without having her dignity undermined by a very visible spill in the parking lot. At least she could blame her fall on the ice, saving herself the embarrassment of tripping over her own feet or nothing at all.

*Calm down,* she told herself. Her nerves had been aflutter since the moment Ethan arrived at her door, eager and ready to attend church.

During the short drive to church, they'd chatted about work, and though Dana didn't like to think about her job on weekends, she felt relieved that the topic of conversation hadn't been more personal.

Torn between wanting their relationship to be more, yet wishing she still had her old position at work, Dana couldn't quite put her finger on how she felt about Ethan. The same went for him asking to attend church this morning. Did he really just need a good church to attend or did some part of him want to spend more time with her?

Not knowing how he felt was the hard part. The easy part was having Ethan hold her arm firmly as they entered the church. Even if they were only friends, she could still pretend they were something more. Her pretending lasted all of fifteen seconds.

"Hi, Aunt Dana." Seventeen-year-old Otis Jr. stopped directly in front of Dana and Ethan. Junior, as the rest of the family called him, gave Ethan the once over, then shifted his gaze back to Dana, plainly curious as to the stranger's identity.

Dana quickly introduced her nephew and Ethan, adding, "He came to work for the Gradys recently and wanted to visit different churches, so I invited him to come here."

Apparently satisfied with this explanation, Junior shook hands with Ethan, then disappeared into the throng of people.

"Your nephew, huh?" Ethan said.

Dana nodded. "The first grandbaby. I was the only aunt in the third grade," she added, laughing.

Ethan gestured in the direction her nephew had disappeared. "*Grandbaby*? He's an inch taller than I am," he said, laughing. "He looks like an ad for a protein drink—you know, the ones that say, 'Drink this, and you'll look like a bodybuilder in a week.' "

"He's the star of his high school football team," added Dana, "and built exactly like my brother, Otis. We're not sure how that happened. My mom is shorter than I am, and my dad is a few inches taller, but both of them are as skinny as beanpoles."

"So Otis is your oldest brother?"

"Yeah," said Dana. "But he's a nice guy."

Ethan let out a mock shudder. "I'm just glad this isn't one

of those moments like in the movies where I meet your entire family for the first time, and we announce we're getting married."

Dana laughed but sobered quickly. "Well, you're partially right."

Ethan shot her a quizzical look. "Partially?"

"Yes, partially. My whole family goes to this church, and they'll want to meet you; but, like you said, we're just friends, so they won't be extremely critical."

"Your whole family?" Ethan repeated.

Dana nodded.

Ethan stood still. "What do you mean by extremely critical?"

Dana shrugged. "It doesn't matter. We're just friends so relax."

Ethan wiggled his eyebrows, looking very much like a mischievous schoolboy. "Suppose I meet them today as your 'friend,' but by this time next week, we decide we're in love and want to be married. Would I have to 'meet' them all over again?"

Dana swatted his arm with the church bulletin. "To be perfectly honest, that scenario has never occurred, as far as I know. We'd be the first."

"Then I'd better get on their good sides now. You never know what the future may hold."

Dana didn't know whether he was still joking or somewhat serious. She didn't have much time to think about the idea because they had entered the sanctuary. Her sister, Latrice, caught sight of her and began gesturing for Dana to come over to the pews the Edwards clan occupied.

"That's my family," Dana told Ethan as they headed closer. From the way everyone's attention focused on Dana and Ethan, she guessed Junior had already reported that she had brought a "friend" with her this morning.

"The whole pew?"

"All three of those pews," she corrected.

"Wow!"

Because the service would begin shortly, Dana made a quick round of introductions. Everyone was obviously interested in knowing exactly who Ethan was, but thankfully, the organ music began, signaling that church had started. Their curiosity would have to wait until later. Because she arrived later than usual, she and Ethan had to squeeze in on the third pew, right next to Junior and his sister, Annitra.

The service lasted a little over two hours, during which Dana's assorted relatives turned and cast what they probably thought were surreptitious glances at her and Ethan. She had the feeling her mother would invite Ethan to Sunday dinner, and she didn't know if that would be a good idea.

They would undoubtedly be somewhat disappointed when they learned she and Ethan weren't dating, but if they liked him well enough, they might get the idea to "help" her and Ethan along into something more. Not only would that be embarrassing for her, but Ethan would wind up feeling totally uncomfortable.

After church ended, Dana had no choice but to finish making the round of introductions to the rest of her family and several curious friends who wanted to meet the visitor. Although Ethan seemed to be handling the attention well, she felt guilty for not having given him more warning about the interest his presence would create.

Her parents, who still hadn't formally met Ethan, were across the sanctuary chatting with a neighbor, and Dana decided she would try to get Ethan out to the car before they had the chance to invite him to dinner. She could rush home and get him back to his car, then make it to Mom and Dad's alone.

Unfortunately, she and Ethan were not of the same mind. He either didn't catch her hints that they needed to leave, or he was flat out ignoring her by talking sports with Otis and Jackson. When she finally managed to convince him that she needed to leave, they exited the sanctuary, only to run right into the Gradys.

"There you are!" Mr. Grady exclaimed. "It's good to see you this morning, Ethan."

Ethan's grin expressed his pleasure at having so easily found a church to attend. "I knew I couldn't go wrong when Dana told me that you attend here as well."

"Does that mean you'll be coming back?" asked Mrs. Grady.

"I think so," Ethan said with a smile. "Everyone I've met has made me feel so welcome. In fact, I'll probably have a hard time leaving when my work here is done."

"We'll miss you too, Ethan," said Mrs. Grady.

This topic caught Dana off guard for a moment. He was right. This church family was warm and close-knit, and Ethan fit in like a long-lost friend. The church members wouldn't be the only ones to miss him when he left. While his absence might return things to normal at work, she wondered if it would also leave an emptiness in her heart.

"We're heading out to dinner soon," said Mr. Grady. "Would you two be interested in joining us?"

"Oh, no you don't." Dana didn't have to turn around to match the good-natured voice to a face.

Dana's mother and father had apparently overheard the Gradys extend the invitation to dinner. "Phil and Nora, I'll have to ask you to take that invitation back. I've cooked plenty for the rest of the family, and I want Dana and her friend here to come and eat with us today," announced her mother. "Of course," she added, smiling, "you two are more than welcome to come too."

Phil and Nora nodded. "That sounds like a good idea to me," said Mr. Grady. "I never turn down good home cooking on a Sunday afternoon."

"Great," said her father. "We'll be glad to have you." He turned to Dana and Ethan. "Young man, I don't think we've met yet." He reached out to shake Ethan's hand.

"Mom and Dad, this is Ethan Miles. Ethan, these are my parents, Mavis and Claude Edwards. Ethan is the new chef I told you about last week. I'm helping him with the menu changes at work."

"Oh, yes," said her father, recognition spreading over his features.

Ethan shook hands with both of her parents and laughed. "Actually, Dana and I are approaching this as more of a joint project."

Dana lifted her eyebrows. She didn't ever remember hearing her job described in this light, even if he had worked hard to keep peace between them at work. Was this a bit of a show for the Gradys and her parents? To her surprise, he continued.

"And I've got a hunch that if Dana told you all about me last week, I might not have gotten a glowing review; but I've had all week to make up for past wrongs, and I think I'm doing a pretty good job." He turned and casually put his arm around Dana.

Her parents gave him a tentative smile, while the Gradys beamed. Dana felt like melting into the floor. This man had just blatantly flirted with her in front of their boss and her parents. . .in a church of all places!

Without being too obvious, Dana gently eased away from his touch. Had he lost his senses? He had all but declared they were in a dating relationship, when they really weren't. Now she knew she had to get him out of the building before he did any more damage.

"You know, I don't know if Ethan is free to come this afternoon," she said, hoping he would take the hint. "Didn't you say you were going to be going over recipes this afternoon?" she asked in a last, and probably desperate-sounding, attempt.

Ethan blinked, looking innocent and confused. "Well, yes, but that won't take me all day. Besides, are you going to dinner?"

Dana sighed. "Yes, I am, but I didn't think you would be interested."

He shook his head and cast a magnanimous smile at her. "I'd hate for you to have to drive all the way back to your place to get me to my car, then have to head back to your parents' house. I'll just come with you to make it easier." As if that weren't enough, he added, "We rode here together," for the benefit of Dana's parents and the Gradys.

Phil, Nora, Mom, and Dad all exchanged glances. Dana knew that look. It could be interpreted as the this-boy-is-serious-about-this-girl look. Under other circumstances, she wouldn't have minded the look; but since Ethan's apparent interest had seemingly "blossomed" within the last few minutes, she couldn't help being a little suspicious.

"Oh. Okay," she said, feeling defeated. Dana didn't doubt that by the time they actually arrived at her parents', the whole house would be abuzz with the account of his apparent attraction to her. She hadn't seen much of Albert and Anthony today, but she wondered if they would be able to place Ethan as the owner of the mysterious gloves from the other night.

"Well, then we'd better get going," she told Ethan.

"The same goes for me," said Mom. "Reverend Brown and his wife will be joining us too, so I've got to run home and get this show on the road. We'll see you there," she said before heading away, Dad right behind her.

The Gradys said their temporary good-byes and left, mentioning they wanted to talk to one of the Sunday school teachers about something.

Dana didn't stop to talk to anyone else but made her way to the parking lot, Ethan hurrying along behind her. As soon as they were in the car, away from curious eyes and ears, she turned to him, ready to give him a piece of her mind. "What in the world were you thinking?" she asked, not sure if his explanation would cause her to laugh or cry.

※

Ethan couldn't quite pin down the meaning of the look on Dana's face. It wavered somewhere between laughter and tears. He felt certain he had done something to distress her and tried not to sound antagonistic. "What do you mean?"

Dana let out a sarcastic laugh. "Are you kidding me? I'm talking about that whole act you put on in front of my parents and the Gradys. What is going on?"

Ethan wasn't exactly sure, himself. Maybe he *had* laid on the charm a little too thick. Maybe not. What he did know was that he liked his new job, his employers, this church, and all of the people he'd met there. Maybe most importantly, he liked Dana.

Of course, he'd not yet told her about this new detail. But then, he too had been hard-pressed to understand this growing attraction he felt. When he arrived at her house this morning, he'd been prepared to be patient—and give her time to decide how she felt about him. At least, that had been his original plan; but when he realized he would get to meet nearly her entire family, he decided he needed to meet them as a man who was interested in her—not merely a friend or coworker. First impressions were important, and he didn't want to spoil his chance with the Edwards family. He had gone wrong by not making Dana aware of how he felt, and he could understand how she would be confused. She apparently thought he had made a major mess of things.

A glance at Dana confirmed that she still waited for his explanation. Ethan took a deep breath, still wondering exactly where he should start.

"I'm sorry. I just wanted to make a good impression on your family, and I got carried away."

Dana gave him a look that spoke volumes—she wouldn't let him off the hook so easily. Would telling her his feelings right now be a good idea? They'd only met a little over a week ago, and that wasn't enough time to go around proclaiming to have fallen in love with someone.

One or both of them could end up hurt if he spoke too soon. For all he knew, she could be in love with someone else. Or he might realize two hours from now that his feelings for her weren't as strong as he'd thought them to be.

He sighed deeply. The only option would be to keep his mouth shut and see how things developed. "Look, I'm really sorry," he tried to explain. "I just messed up. Will you forgive me?"

Her features softened somewhat. "I guess so," she said after a moment. "But now my whole family will be expecting to hear that we're actually dating or something like that."

"Something like what?" Ethan tried to lighten the mood.

Dana's face relaxed a tiny bit more, and Ethan guessed she might be less upset than she had been minutes earlier.

"We don't have to disappoint them, you know. We are dating," Ethan interrupted. "Sort of," he said with a shrug.

Dana gave him a blank look.

"Remember? Dinner the other night? And lunch together nearly every day?" He searched her face carefully for any sign that she had enjoyed their time away from work together as much as he had.

Dana spoke again, her voice laced with caution. "Every time we went somewhere, you always mentioned how you were getting a lot of research done for your future restaurant, or you called it a working lunch. You never said we were dating, and you certainly didn't act like we were dating."

Ethan felt like his heart had gone tumbling down the stairwell of a ten-story building. Sure, he'd tried to give the impression that they were going out on business, but surely she realized after a few days that they weren't really discussing business during those times together.

While he contemplated how he should reply to this latest comment, Dana started the car. "Forget it," she told him. "If we don't get there soon, they'll have to wait dinner for us. Trust me, you might have made a good impression on my brothers this morning, but if you hold up dinner, they won't be amused."

Ethan wanted to finish the conversation, but it seemed Dana wanted to drop the subject, so he felt content to let the topic rest for the time being.

The street in front of Claude and Mavis's home was lined with cars on both sides. "Did I happen to come on family reunion Sunday?"

She laughed and shook her head. "No, it's like this every week. The whole family, and whatever friends and neighbors Mom and Dad invite, converge on the house every Sunday after church and stay for the afternoon."

Ethan got out of the car and hurried around to open her door. While they walked to the house, he casually reached out and took hold of her hand. As they had been the night he and Dana had gone to dinner together, her small hands were cold. He'd loan her his gloves, except she hadn't yet returned them. He wanted to tease her about still having his gloves, but he didn't want to ruin the moment.

This marked the first time he and Dana had truly held hands. They'd brushed fingers on occasion, and this morning he'd briefly held her hand as he helped her up from her fall on the ice, but he now reached out with the intention of staying connected with her. To his surprise, she didn't pull away from him.

Instead she gave him a relaxed smile. "You've done it now, you know. I can tell you that at least one person inside that house has noted the fact that we're holding hands."

"So?" Ethan asked, not willing to let go. Her hand fit his perfectly. The simple act didn't feel awkward or forced, but totally comfortable. He hoped this could be a sign of a possible change in the way she felt about him and, ultimately, about *them*.

"So they'll be talking about it. Wondering. Asking questions."

Ethan shrugged. "I don't mind, if you don't."

Dana didn't say anything, but she didn't remove her hand from his. Surely more than chance had put them together. He remembered the first day he had seen her, just over a week ago. She'd intrigued him from the start, and he'd prayed for the opportunity to meet her again. To his surprise, he had. Talk about answered prayer!

A nagging thought popped into his head. Would the Lord have answered his prayer, only to show him that he and Dana weren't meant for each other? The idea seemed unlikely and even borderline cruel, but Ethan wasn't willing to take a chance on pushing God out of the picture just because things were going well at the moment.

*Lord, am I moving too fast for Your will?* he prayed as they stepped inside of the Edwards household. *Am I doing the right thing?*

❧

*Lord, this feels right. But am I getting ahead of You?* Dana prayed as she and Ethan stepped inside the house. Holding

Ethan's hand felt. . .she couldn't describe the feeling with one word. "Right" was too cliché. "Comfortable" was too bland. "Nice" was too unimaginative.

Whatever this indescribable feeling eventually turned out to be, she hated to see it end, but she had to let go of his hand in order to help her mom and the other women get dinner on the table. The sound of the men and boys laughing and teasing echoed from the direction of the living room, while the clanging of pots and pans rang out from the kitchen.

Holding Ethan's hand might be nice, but if the two of them stood in the front hallway for much longer, the entire family would be making jokes at their expense. Dana gave Ethan a little squeeze to let him know she didn't want to run away from him, then let go.

"I've got to help out in the kitchen, but you can stay here and talk with the guys."

Ethan nodded, and Dana steered him in the direction of the living room. As soon as they came to the doorway, Mr. Grady and a few of the others called for him to come join them.

Once she felt Ethan was settled, Dana headed to the kitchen to lend her help. Her mother usually did most of the cooking, although many times her sisters and sisters-in-law brought a dish or two.

Her sister, Sheryl, took the lead in peppering her with questions about Ethan.

"Isn't that the same guy you complained would undermine your position at work?"

Mrs. Grady, in the corner buttering rolls, looked surprised to hear this. "I didn't know you felt like that, Honey."

Dana cringed inwardly. Didn't Sheryl realize she couldn't just blurt things out when her boss's wife stood nearby? Since everyone seemed to be waiting for her answer, she nodded. "Yes, he is the same guy, but things at work haven't been as bad as I thought." Silently, she added, *Of course, things could have been better, but no way am I going to let Mrs. Grady think I'm whining.*

Dana's admission that things weren't so terrible after all brought on gales of laughter from the others.

"I'll say," said Verna, Otis's wife. "He's not bad on the eyes either."

Dana had to smile. Her family members always teased and joked around with each other like this. Over the years, she had done her fair share of teasing. Her moment to be on the receiving end of the ribbing had come, so she couldn't get upset.

"Really, you guys, we've only known each other a little over a week," she explained. "So don't get carried away."

"I fell in love with Donald in a week," supplied her sister, Latrice.

"Ahem. . . ," said Aunt Florence. "The first time you clapped eyes on Donald, you were in the first grade. If you're younger than eighteen, it doesn't count."

Everyone burst out laughing again, pausing long enough for Latrice to defend herself. "Speak for yourself—but mind you, I never said he fell in love with me that same week."

"Yes," said Aunt Daphne. "But what was the boy supposed to do, what with you chasing after him all those years?"

"Umm-hmm," added Florence. "By the time you graduated from college, the boy just got plumb wore out. He married you because that was the only way he could get a break."

Latrice playfully tossed a dishtowel at Florence, then hugged the woman.

While everyone laughed at the latest exchange between Latrice and Florence, Dana took advantage of her moment off of the hot seat to grab a stack of plates and head to the dining room to set the table.

There were actually several tables of varying sizes and

shapes packed into the oversized dining room, and Dana couldn't remember a time they only had just one table in use for Sunday dinner.

Years ago, a new neighbor had made a snide comment about the "disheveled décor" in the room.

Mom, not missing a beat, had answered that she collected tables and chairs like some people collected dolls or coins. She then asserted that her collection might be more useful because they helped make room for friends and family.

"Whenever I get a new table, I never seem to have any trouble finding people to come over and sit down to dinner," she had told the woman, effectively putting an end to the topic.

Now that woman attended on Sundays at least once a month, and she never complained of not having a good time, despite the so-called disheveled décor.

The huge Victorian style house had been built nearly ninety years ago, and large rooms were one of the greatest advantages of the place. Her mother always seemed to find new spots to put things, and while the furnishings needed some updating, the interior was a comfortable jumble of the things her parents loved and refused to part with. And while Mom and Dad sometimes grew weary with the constant upkeep on the house, they liked the charm of the place and refused to move away.

Of course, her parents were more apt to keep the house as long as Latrice and her family lived just next door. Having someone reliable nearby gave Dana and her siblings tremendous comfort.

Albert and Anthony were the last to leave the nest. Still, Dana and her siblings visited their parents quite frequently. Daughters, daughters-in-law, and granddaughters helped Mom with the interior, while sons, sons-in-law, and grandsons helped Dad with the exterior.

Someday, Dana hoped for the opportunity to bring her own little ones to visit Grandma and Grandpa. A wave of wistfulness washed over her. While her sisters had married and begun families with ease, the mysterious path leading toward her own husband still remained stubbornly hidden.

Her thoughts were interrupted when her sisters entered the room, bringing food to place on the tables. In a matter of minutes, everything was in place for dinner to begin.

After everyone assembled in the dining room, Dad prayed over the meal, and the assortment of guests sat down to dinner.

Dana and Ethan sat at a small, square table with the Gradys, and to her dismay, most of the conversation revolved around work. All traces of the sentimental man who gently held her hand just an hour ago disappeared during the discussion. He had been replaced with Ethan-the-Chef.

When the Gradys expressed concern over whether or not customers would eat bagels flavored with beets and saffron, Ethan-the-Chef actually had the nerve to tell them he really needed complete control of the project to make it a success. "I know what people like," he assured them. "I've done this dozens of times, and I really do think I have the recipe for success." Smiling, he added, "No pun intended."

His voice carried a tone of absolute confidence that irked Dana more and more as the meal progressed. What made him so certain he could waltz into town and, in a little over seven days, decide what the customers would and wouldn't like?

Dana felt that as the district manager, she had a better idea of what the customers would like. And while they might not be storming the store to pick up loaves of oatmeal wheat bread, her intuition told her that saffron-beet bagels would probably send them *running* to The Loaf.

Ethan's problem came from the fact that he had yet to go out and talk to a customer. Dana spent her fair share of time at the main office behind a desk, but she'd put in a good many hours behind the counter as well. She thrived with the hands-on approach. Ethan liked to create from feeling and ideas.

When he mentioned he had an idea to put basil and mint in the house cornbread recipe, Dana decided he had gone far enough.

This had gotten downright ridiculous. There needed to be a balance between his creativity and her sensibility, or one of them would get frustrated. . .and that someone would likely be her, since Ethan considered himself the authority on projects like this.

"I have an idea," Dana said before she could lose her nerve. The three of them turned to face Dana, who had been largely silent during the conversation.

"Yes, Dear?" said Mrs. Grady.

Dana suddenly felt self-conscious. How could she say this without attacking Ethan's creativity or sounding like she needed to defend her ego? "Well. . .I just wondered if we might be moving along too quickly. Or maybe even taking drastic steps we don't need to take."

"How so?" asked Mr. Grady.

"For instance, this mint and basil cornbread. Do you really think people are going to love it?"

Mr. Grady shrugged. "I like plain food myself, so it doesn't appeal to me. But Ethan's right about folks nowadays wanting to eat fancier dishes. I think we'd lose more ground to the competition if we didn't compete."

"But The Loaf has plain cornbread with a fancy name," Dana countered. "Maybe people just like the name. What if they hate our mint basil cornbread? What if they stop coming because we added too many distracting ingredients to everything on the menu?"

Ethan cleared his throat. "Dana, I've really tried to be

patient, but just because you want things to stay the same doesn't mean the Gradys do. They've hired me to help change things, so if I left things as they are, I'd be letting them down and taking their money for no reason."

Dana bit her lip. He had a point, but then, so did she. She looked to Mr. Grady for help. He, himself, had admitted that Ethan's recipes sounded a little far out for his taste.

Mr. Grady looked torn for a moment. Finally, he spoke. "I wish I had something to offer, but I don't. I've lost touch with what people want, and that's why I hired Ethan." Almost regretfully, he turned to Dana. "I've got too much money tied up in this to just give up and leave things the same."

Dana felt like the wind had been knocked out of her. Mr. Grady had sided with Ethan and basically told her to mind her own business.

"I think I have a suggestion," said Ethan. "Maybe we should set some boundaries. I know I said I needed an assistant in developing and testing the recipes, but maybe things would go smoother if I could work with someone else. That way Dana could get back to her old job."

Mr. Grady nodded cautiously. "Sure, I think we could do that. But when it's time to get the food to the stores, you'll still need to let Dana know how you're progressing, since she's in charge of the other managers. She'll need to have a fair lead time to work with the advertising department to get the word out. Then she'll need to know how you want to phase things in so the employees in the stores will be ready."

"That works for me," said Ethan. Looking at Dana, he asked, "How about you?"

Despite the fact that she still didn't like Ethan's approach, Dana felt satisfied with this arrangement. She was back in charge again, and Ethan would have to find another assistant. "Works for me," Dana said cheerily.

Before they could discuss things further, they were interrupted when Otis Junior came to the table, balancing four small plates with pieces of Mom's famous, gooey butter cake.

"This is delicious," said Ethan, taking a bite. Laughing, he added, "Is this a St. Louis specialty?"

Mrs. Grady laughed. "You could say that. It's pretty popular here, but everyone has her own twist on how to make it."

Dana bit into her cake, but the pieces felt like sand in her mouth. She knew she should feel victorious at having the opportunity to go back to her old routine. No more early mornings watching Ethan measure flour and chop herbs. No more writing down different ingredients when he got an idea. No more being called the assistant.

But that also meant no more workdays spent at Ethan's side. Had this decision been a win or a loss?

# eight

Two weeks later, Dana arrived at work a little earlier than usual. The kitchen remodel at the main office had finally been completed, and that meant Ethan would be able to move his testing facility away from the other kitchens where people actually worked.

On her way to her own office, she took a detour by way of the kitchen to see if Ethan had arrived. Truth be told, she was excited to see him. Ever since their decision to work separately, she had not seen much of him. Apparently, he'd been spending every spare moment testing recipes and had actually started working from the kitchen at his condo because there he wouldn't get in anyone's way. The only exception to this was church on Sundays. But he now drove his own car instead of them riding together as they had done that first Sunday. And while he came to dinner at her parents' after services, he tended to spend a lot of time talking with her father and brothers, especially Albert and Anthony.

This abrupt interruption of their time together had also pushed aside any inkling of what had seemed to be a budding relationship between them, and Dana wondered if she had imagined that he had ever held her hand. Their conversation in the car about whether or not they were really dating didn't even matter anymore. How could dating be an issue between two people who rarely even saw each other?

❧

Dana didn't know where their relationship stood, but she wanted to find out. Waiting in the hallway outside of the test kitchen, she could see Ethan through the large plate glass windows. He kneaded dough, while his assistant dutifully chopped some greenish herb.

Not wanting to interrupt, Dana tapped on the window to get his attention. He looked up, not missing a beat in the constant motion of kneading. With a smile and quick nod of his head, he motioned for her to come inside.

Dana opened the door and walked in. Something smelled a little. . .odd, but she decided not to mention it. There would be no sense in starting an unnecessary argument with him.

"I wasn't sure you were here, but I guess I should have known you'd already be hard at work by now," she said cheerily.

His laugh reminded Dana of how much she had missed seeing him every day. She took another step toward the table where he worked. She wanted to talk to him but didn't want to yell across the room so his assistant would hear every word.

He must have understood her reticence. "Andrea, why don't you go ahead and take that coffee break?"

The young woman smiled gratefully, and Dana returned the smile, remembering the few days she'd worked with Ethan in the kitchen. The man had boundless energy. He liked to start work before the sun came up and continued working well into the night hours. Ethan was the only person Dana knew who would fit the description of both an early bird and a night owl.

"Haven't seen you in awhile," said Ethan. He shaped the dough he'd been working into a round ball and put it aside.

"I know. We've been working too hard, I guess."

He moved toward a cooling rack where several loaves of bread rested. "I want you to taste something."

Dana nodded and waited while he cut a slice of still-warm bread. She chewed and swallowed. The bread didn't taste bad, but whatever he put in it made it hot—as in spicy. Dana had tasted chili that didn't burn this much.

Ethan waited for her opinion with an expectant look on his face. "What do you think?"

Dana grimaced, fanning her mouth. "It's spicy."

Ethan grinned. "I know. Cayenne, mustard, and anise. Do you like it?"

She shrugged. "I'm sure someone will. I'm sorry I can't be more helpful, but I just don't care for spicy food."

"Oh." He put the bread away, while Dana fixed herself a glass of water.

"I just wanted to see how things were going with the new recipes," Dana told him. "Mr. Grady mentioned that you were ready to get some into the stores."

"Yes, that's right," said Ethan. "Why don't we discuss this at lunch?"

"That's fine with me. I'll be free after twelve-thirty or so."

"Then I'll come up to your office and get you when I'm ready."

"Okay, I'll see you then." As Dana left the kitchen, she couldn't keep the smile off her face. Now that she and Ethan had spent some time away from each other, it seemed that their friendship had gotten back on track.

❧

Ethan knocked on the door to Dana's office.

"Come on in," she called.

He entered to find her at her desk on the phone. She motioned for him to sit down. While she talked, Ethan waited patiently for her to finish her conversation. Apparently, she spoke to someone in the advertising department about how to introduce the new menu items.

Ethan realized he did feel a bit impatient for their lunch meeting to begin. While he supposed it had been a good idea for them to work at their own separate jobs, he hadn't realized just how much he would miss Dana. Seeing her on Sundays had come to be the highlight of his week, and now that they were beginning the next phase of the project, they would be able to spend more time together. Of course, the closer they moved to the completion of the job, the closer he came to leaving for another assignment.

Dana finally hung up the phone, and minutes later, they were on their way to a nearby café.

During their discussion, Ethan told Dana about the recipes he wanted to introduce first. He sensed she still had issues about the flavors being too unusual, and it disturbed him. He was in charge of the creation process, and her job was to get his food into the stores. Knowing that she didn't totally agree with his ideas still bothered him.

He'd poured his heart into his recipes. If Dana didn't accept his work, it would feel like she rejected a part of him.

Ethan blew out a sigh. There was obviously something about him she didn't like or trust. He'd sensed it from their first meeting with the Gradys. Although she hadn't said exactly what upset her, until the issue got out in the open, there would be no way their friendship could grow stronger. He decided to ask her exactly what was going on before it grew too late.

"Dana, I'm getting the feeling that you don't like something about me or my work," he said. Dana looked at him with surprise, but she didn't object, confirming his feelings. "Now I know we're working toward the same goal here, but this sidestepping the issue has to stop. What is going on?"

She didn't answer right away. After a long pause, she nodded. "Okay, but not here. There's a lot to this, and I don't have time to go into all of the details right now."

Ethan shook his head. "I don't think it will be good for the company if we wait much longer. I almost get the feeling sometimes that we're working against each other instead of with each other."

"I do too," she answered. "But really, I think it would be better if we waited until after work. I've got a million things on my to-do list for today. So could we talk about this tonight?"

"I can't tonight. I'm going to the Gradys' for dinner, but I'm free tomorrow night. How about then?"

"I can't. I'm babysitting for Jackson and Marva."

"Wednesday?"

Dana shrugged. "That might work. But I'm supposed to help with the youth group at church. They're rehearsing for the Easter play, and I'm the assistant director. Afterward, I'm going to Mom and Dad's for late dinner, so you're welcome to come along. Maybe we can talk on the way there."

Ethan's spirits lifted when Dana extended the invitation. She seemed relieved that he wanted to get this conversation out of the way. Maybe then they could move forward with their friendship. "Wednesday it is. Maybe we could go out for a bite to eat after work. I'll be starving if I have to wait that long for dinner."

Dana laughed. "To tell you the truth, I'm usually pretty hungry by then too. How about you get to my house at five, then we can get food and be at the church by six-thirty?"

"Perfect."

Just then, the waitress came with the check, and Dana insisted on paying. "I have cash with me today."

After paying the bill, they headed outdoors to Ethan's car. While they rode, Ethan debated asking Dana out on an "official" date. His new next-door neighbor was an actress and had given him a free pair of tickets to her newest play, set to premiere Friday at a local theater. At first he'd refused the tickets, since he wasn't especially interested in theater; but when she'd persisted, he'd accepted, thinking he might be able to persuade Dana to go with him.

Now his plan had hit a snag, since he'd wanted to get their work discussion out of the way before pursuing any type of romantic relationship with her. The play opened two days after their conversation would take place. If he asked Wednesday night, he'd be risking the chance that she'd already have plans. He wondered if Dana was one of those women who flat out refused a date if the guy didn't give at least a week's notice. If he asked now, and the conversation on Wednesday didn't go well, then he'd have the unpleasant task of backing out on the date, something he felt would be tacky.

As Ethan mulled over the options, Dana spoke up, interrupting his strategy planning session. "Ethan? I need to ask you something."

"Sure."

"I may be doing this all wrong, but I'm a little confused. Sometimes I get the feeling we're heading toward a more than friendship-type of relationship, and sometimes it feels like we barely know each other. I guess I want to know if you're feeling the same way."

He exhaled softly. "I do, but if we get into that, we'll have to open that can of worms you wanted to put off until Wednesday night."

They had reached the parking lot of the Grady's main office, and Ethan pulled into an empty space. "I'll tell you what I feel, and you can decide if we should finish this conversation later as well."

Dana frowned slightly, small wrinkles forming above her brows. "Okay, I think I know where you're heading with this, and I think we shouldn't put it off. How much time do you have right now?"

He shrugged. "I'm flexible, but I thought you had a desk overflowing with stuff to do."

"It can wait a little while," she said. "So let's talk."

"Okay. To make a long story short, I'm interested in a romantic relationship with you. I felt attracted to you when we met in line at The Loaf. I got the feeling that you felt the same way. I hoped we'd run into each other again, and I prayed about it. I was so glad to see you that night at dinner, but you treated me like. . ." Ethan trailed off, unable to put his thoughts into words. "I just got the impression that you were upset with me."

Dana didn't answer right away, but when she spoke, her words poured out. "You're right; I did get upset. I'll be honest with you. Ever since I was a little girl, my family has gone to Grady Bakeries. I worked there as a clerk in high school. I worked as an assistant manger during my last two years of college. After I graduated, they promoted me to be the manager of one of the stores. Then, last year, I got this promotion.

"First of all, I worried that your being here and my having to be your assistant made it seem like my opinion didn't matter. I felt like I'd been demoted.

"I've worked hard for this job, and the thought of the company going out of business scares me." She shook her head, then continued. "Really, I'm not trying to work against you. But I feel like we have to be careful in how we go about changing the Grady Bakery image. I like your creativity, and I like most of your recipes—but that's beside the point."

Dana grinned and placed her hand on top of his. "Face it, Ethan, you're probably the only person who's going to like all of your recipes. You shouldn't take that as a personal offense."

Ethan chuckled. "Am I that transparent?"

Dana quirked an eyebrow and grinned. "Actually, I just guessed. This is my whole point: I know you probably think I'm fighting tooth and nail to discourage you, but I'm the last person who wants the bakeries to close. I love my job.

"We're not some fancy gourmet place, and we've never pretended we were—at least, not until now. We're just an organic bakery that has been around for years and years. We've done well selling simple, wholesome, tasty foods, and it's worked for us. Sure, the customers haven't been as faithful as they have been in the past, but that's no reason to alienate the ones who still like the menu exactly the way it is. I'm convinced that our problem doesn't have one all-encompassing explanation.

"Lack of variety plays a part, but things change. Customers move away. Maybe people have forgotten about Grady Bakeries. Or maybe new folks in town don't even know about us. I don't think we've explored these avenues enough." She shrugged, then grew silent.

Ethan had to admit that Dana had a point, but this was not his territory. He'd assumed these points had been covered long before he'd come on the scene. What did she expect him to do about it? He couldn't very well tell the Gradys to fire him, try other options, then contact him later if they didn't work.

He shook his head and looked into Dana's eyes. She was obviously upset; near the verge of tears. "Okay, I see your point—but what am I supposed to do about it? I'm here to do a job, and I can't not do what they've asked me to."

Dana wiped a tear away from her cheek with the back of her hand, leaving a trail of mascara on the side of her face. Then, a steady stream of tears began to fall.

Ethan didn't know what to do. He hadn't expected her to break down like this. "Don't cry," he said, fumbling around in his jacket pocket for a tissue. After locating a clean handkerchief, he gave it to Dana.

She accepted it and proceeded to bury her face in the cloth as she continued to weep. After a few moments, she looked up from the handkerchief. "What if your 'recipe for success' fails? Then what happens? The Gradys will have to close the bakery, and I'll lose my job—and so will everyone else," she said between sobs. "But that won't matter to you. You'll be off at your next job, trying out your recipes until you decide to open your own restaurant."

Ethan felt helpless and somewhat defensive. She had all but accused him of doing only what he wanted instead of coming up with something that would work for the Gradys.

Still, no matter how much he wanted to brush off Dana's concerns, he couldn't totally ignore her point. Although she had never done his job, he supposed maybe he sometimes did put his ideas ahead of the agenda for this job.

There remained the possibility that he had been right, and Dana was wrong. Then again, maybe she'd been right, and he stood in the wrong. Judging from past experience, Ethan guessed that neither one of them was one hundred percent correct, and the solution most likely lay somewhere in the middle. The only way to find out would be to get the new breads into the stores and see how the customers reacted.

Ethan started to say so but bit back the words, realizing Dana would probably take his observation as a challenge.

There needed to be a way to let the customers decide—but how? His job required him to get the food into the restaurants, then his work would be done. He hadn't planned to stick around to see how things went after the fact.

As he mulled this over, a glimmer of an idea took root in his mind and started to grow. Turning to Dana, he put his plan into words. "What if we introduced the new foods but didn't set anything in stone?"

"What?"

"What I mean is, we can do surveys, have the customers fill out opinion sheets, things like that. If one recipe seems to be a total failure, we ditch it or tweak it. If they get totally disgusted that one of the old breads is missing, then we bring it back."

A hopeful look crossed Dana's face for a millisecond, then disappeared. "But that will take time and more money because we'll need more employees to do the surveys. I doubt Mr. Grady will go for that."

Ethan considered her words for a moment. Dana was right; the Gradys didn't have the money or time this would take. Unless. . .

"What if you and I do the work? I could stick around for an extra month or so and not charge any additional fees. If you can rearrange your schedule, you and I can rotate between the three stores, conduct surveys, and find out exactly what people think of the new menu."

"And then what?" Dana had stopped crying and folded the handkerchief.

Ethan looked her in the eye. "We do what it takes to get business thriving again. I promise I won't leave until I get it right. I'll do everything I can to keep the Grady Bakeries alive." As he spoke the words, a weight like a rock settled in Ethan's stomach. Was this plan too ambitious? What if this company was really on its last leg? Then what would he do?

"Really?" The light returned to Dana's eyes. "You promise?"

Ethan swallowed. He might be in way over his head, but right now, reassuring Dana mattered the most. "I promise," said Ethan.

Dana smiled. "Then I have work to do. I should probably get back to the office." She sounded almost apologetic.

Ethan cleared his throat. "So should I."

Once inside the building, before they went their separate ways, Dana held up his handkerchief. "I don't suppose you want this back right now?"

"No, I don't think so. Since we're still on for Wednesday, you can give it back to me then."

"Sure." Dana hesitated. "But I thought we just had the big discussion."

Ethan shrugged. "So, who says we can't hang out? I mean, is there any reason that you don't want us to get to know each other better?"

Dana looked him in the eye yet didn't speak right away. "I don't exactly hate the idea. Still, I don't think we should get too serious since you're not planning to stick around after everything is in place here."

"Okay," Ethan said, trying to look cheerful. He guessed she had taken the logical point of view, but he didn't feel too happy about it. "So. . .you're saying that we can only be friends?"

Dana looked at her shoes, then somewhere behind him, just above his head. "I guess so. I mean, both of us are happy with our jobs, and we're pretty settled into our routines." She shrugged. "I guess I'm saying that if we did get serious, we'd have a lot of reorganizing to do. You like New York, and I like St. Louis, so who would have to pack up and move?"

Ethan didn't think her reasoning made much of a difference. After all, wasn't love supposed to conquer all? He couldn't imagine distance being able to suppress true love. He didn't argue. Instead, he gave her a half-hearted nod.

"Okay. If that's how you want to approach things, we'll be friends. But if we start feeling differently, I don't think we should let distance be a factor. There's always the chance that God created us just for each other."

Dana lifted an eyebrow. "So what's your point?"

"My point? God doesn't make mistakes. If He planned something, we're the only ones who can mess up His plan by not doing what He wants us to. So, if He wants us to be together, do you think He's looking down here saying, 'Oops, they live in different cities. Better scratch that one.'"

Dana gave him an incredulous look for a long moment. Then she broke into laughter. Shaking her head, she said, "Okay, you're right. So we'll just spend time together and keep praying to see what the Lord's will is for us. If that means more than friendship, then I won't argue with Him."

"Good. Neither will I," said Ethan.

Dana pointed toward the stairway. "I need to get back to work, so I'll see you. . ."

"Later," Ethan finished.

"Later," said Dana. As she headed for the staircase, she looked over her shoulder. "And I love your idea about the surveys." The smile on her face reminded him of liquid sunshine. "Thanks for sharing it with me. I promise to do my best to make sure it goes well." She gave a little wave and walked upstairs.

Ethan stood watching until she disappeared at the top. "Lord," he said quietly. "I really like her. If I can't help this bakery stay in business, I think she's going to be really upset with me, so I'd appreciate all the help You can give us."

❧

Dana tossed and turned for a long time that night, unable to sleep. Instead, she kept replaying her conversation with Ethan in her mind.

Had her imagination worked overtime, or had they really discussed everything from work to a possible relationship?

Ethan's words about "God creating us for each other," weighed heavily on her mind. Was there such a thing as a perfect mate for anyone?

Dana had no clear answer. Of course, ever since she was in high school and old enough to understand the importance of choosing a good mate, she'd prayed regularly about her future husband.

Some of her friends prayed for God to send them "The One," and Dana had always written them off as people who were too obsessed with fairy tales.

There had been a time when she had looked forward to a fairy tale romance, but the way things had been going lately, she wondered if she would end up perpetually single. That is, before Ethan came along.

She dated off and on, but never seriously. The men she'd gone out with were nice, but not her ideal.

What *was* her ideal? Without a doubt, he was part fairy tale, part romance novel hero. Her freshman year of college, Dana and several of her friends had written down their description of the perfect husband. Dana's hero would be dashingly handsome, gentle, and sensitive, but confident and strong. He would like animals and children and abhor all evil. If the need arose, he would be willing to drop everything just to be there for her.

Of course, *he* had never appeared. And Dana's friends who were now married had eventually marked more than a few qualifications off of their own lists.

Naively, Dana had once shown her list to Latrice, and within twenty-four hours, all of her siblings had heard about it. They had teased her mercilessly, especially the twins. Her mother finally came to her rescue, gently reminding them that they shouldn't make fun of Dana for having high standards but admonishing Dana that God knew what was best for a person, and He would give her the mate He knew she needed.

After three years of carrying that wish list around, Dana finally put it away, even though she could still remember every word of it. After graduating from college, Dana decided that since Mr. Right hadn't come around, she would concentrate on work until he put in an appearance.

She began her career as one treading water; her job served as merely something to do until Mr. Right showed up. In the meantime, she chalked his absence up to reality.

Obviously, life didn't work as smoothly as a fairy tale, so she had to think more practically. And her list of ideals probably needed to be adjusted, not abandoned. After all, it was entirely possible that Prince Charming's horse simply had a broken leg.

After a year or so, she'd given up treading water in favor of a tentative dogpaddle. Mr. Wonderful hadn't yet appeared, and the first promotion had all but fallen in her lap. Another advancement propelled the dogpaddle into a more vigorous motion. Thoughts of Mr. Wonderful had taken a back seat, and Dana perfected a full out breaststroke, moving as one training for the Olympics. Who needed a Mr. Wonderful when she had a medal within her reach?

Things had worked out well until Ethan had appeared. In her opinion, she all but had that medal in the bag. She stood at the top of her game, in a position of authority and prestige. No more treading water, no more dog paddling. Dana was on her way to the podium. Mr. Wonderful would have to catch *her.*

Ethan's arrival had knocked her out of the deep water and back into the shallow kiddie pool, where even treading water was out of the question. No longer the boss, she took directions instead of giving them. Thankfully, Ethan had been wise enough to suggest that she return to her old job while he did his. He still held a position of prestige, but once he returned to New York, she would be able to regain her ground.

Dana punched her pillow, searching for a more comfortable position. "And that's where it gets confusing," she said aloud to the empty bedroom.

Yes, she wanted to be at the top of her game again—but she didn't want Ethan to leave so quickly.

Lately, her thoughts of career were constantly competing with dreams of marriage and family. Dana wondered if this might be some type of internal diversion tactic; a way to disguise her frustration with her change of role at work.

Or might the simple truth lay in the fact that she had fallen for Ethan and didn't care that every minute she spent with him seemed to chip away at her intense career ambition?

She didn't know. She couldn't come up with anything to

compare this feeling with. This certainly wasn't a fairy tale. Or a book. Or a movie.

In the majority of these fictional scenarios, the heroine was tall, thin, and beautiful. Her voice rang out in a flawless soprano, and she never had bad hair days. The hero was handsome, dashing, and brave. He knew exactly what he wanted— the heroine—and nothing stopped him from pursuing her.

Dana's life did not fit that description in the least. At five foot two, the last time she had been tall was at birth, measuring twenty-two inches long. She had been the "tallest" baby in the nursery at the time. And thin was relative. Every few months, she embarked on a new plan that never seemed to get rid of those extra ten pounds. The theory of relativity applied to her hair as well. She'd experimented with many ways to work with the texture God had given her, and currently, the easiest option was to spend several hours in a chair while Latrice painstakingly braided her hair into hundreds of tiny braids.

So, she wasn't the typical heroine, but she had yet to meet the perfect man. While Ethan might be tall and dark, he still wasn't extremely handsome. In addition, he possessed his own puzzling collection of foibles. One minute, he held her hand. The next, he fluffed his ego, bragging about his "recipe for success." Never mind the fact that if customers didn't like his gourmet creations, the Gradys would be back in trouble again. He had obviously missed the day at school when they discussed the Customer is Always Right rule.

Dana shook her head. Sometimes she had the feeling that Ethan couldn't see the forest for the trees. Yet, in an instant, he had reversed her opinion of him with his idea about surveying the customers and his offer to stick around longer to get the job done correctly.

Then, he'd amazed her again, hinting about a possible romantic relationship.

What had happened? Dana didn't know, but she no longer counted down the days until Ethan left. Was there any reason why she shouldn't just relax and see how things developed? The question had only one answer.

"Lord," Dana prayed. "I feel so confused. I'm alternating between feeling like meeting Ethan is the best thing that's happened to me, then wishing I had never met him.

I guess the thing I need to do is stop relying on how I feel and find out what You know. Please show me how I should approach my relationship with Ethan. Should I treat him like a coworker, a good friend, or a future husband?"

# nine

The next morning, while Ethan worked in the test kitchen, Mr. Grady stopped in to speak with him.

"What's this I've been hearing about customer surveys? How much more is this going to cost?"

"Any extra costs will be minimal. Basically, we're only going to need to write up a survey sheet and make copies."

Mr. Grady shook his head. "You never mentioned any surveys before. I thought you had a foolproof plan."

Ethan nodded. "Well, we think it wouldn't hurt to double check. Dana wanted to make sure that the customers really like the new items and find out if we need to bring back some of the older ones. The only way to be certain is to actually ask, so that's what we're going to do."

Mr. Grady gave him a dubious look. "And this is all right with you? I thought you two were working separately."

Ethan waved away the man's concern. "I assure you, we're both in agreement. The reason we're working together is that we know how it needs to be done. Plus, you won't have to hire more people to do it."

Mr. Grady brightened at this new aspect. "Sounds like a good plan to me. Tell Dana congratulations for coming up with such a brilliant plan." With that, he turned and left.

Ethan refrained from correcting the notion that Dana had come up with the plan. It really belonged to him, but he supposed it didn't really make that much of a difference. Who cared who owned the idea, as long as it proved to be helpful?

❧

"Mmm. . ." The woman bit into the scone again. As she chewed, she hummed appreciatively. "Oh, yes, these are really good. Are you going to keep these?"

Dana decided to let Ethan answer that one.

"If they go over with everyone else the same way they have with you, then yes, they'll stay on the menu."

The woman distributed the remainder of the scone between her two children. "Well, I definitely like the Orange Cranberry Raisin scones a lot better than the plain raisin ones you had before. These seem more moist and buttery. I mean, I could serve these at a tea or something."

"Well, thanks so much for your comments," said Dana.

"Oh, it's no problem for me," said the lady. "I just can't wait until you start selling these behind the counter. Do you think it'll be long before you're done testing?"

"No, Ma'am, we don't anticipate longer than a week or two to get an item in the store after it's been tested. Within a couple of months, we should have the entire new menu in place," Ethan explained.

"Good," she said. With that, she shepherded her children away from the sample table and toward the counter to place her order.

A few customers later, Dana looked at her watch. "It's about closing time for us."

Ethan agreed. "Yeah, we only have about half a dozen scones left. Do you want to take them home with you?"

Dana laughed. "No thanks. I've been smelling them all day, so it feels like I've eaten a dozen. Why don't we leave them here for the workers?"

"Good idea."

As Dana gathered up her purse, coat, notebooks, and other work materials, she and Ethan laughed and joked about their day. This had been the third day in a row of testing customer reactions to the new scones, and the decision appeared to be pretty straightforward.

"Looks like the orange scones are here to stay," said Dana.

"Looks that way. Of course, we'll have to check over all of the written surveys to be sure; but if everything goes well, I think I can get the bakers in the kitchen this weekend to teach them how to make these."

"I'll see you in the morning," said Dana. "We're going to be testing the Parmesan tomato bagels, right?"

Right," agreed Ethan. "Are you going anywhere tonight?"

Dana stopped and smiled at him. "Are you asking me out?" Last Wednesday, Ethan had accompanied her to the Easter play practice, and on Friday, they had gone to his next-door neighbor's play. Sunday, he'd come to dinner at her parents' home, and yesterday evening, they had gone to dinner after work.

He grinned. "As a matter of fact, I am. Don't you have to help with the Easter play again tonight?"

"I do. I will every Wednesday until after Easter, but you're welcome to come along."

"I'll meet you at the church," he said. "And while I'm at it, do you have plans for Saturday? I thought we could spend some time together."

Dana shrugged in apology. "I'm being 'Aunt Dana' for the day and taking a few nieces and nephews to the Magic House."

"Magic House?"

"It's a children's museum. They have all kinds of hands on stuff to keep kids busy for the day."

Ethan nodded. "I see. How about Saturday night?"

"We have plans for pizza and that new cartoon at the movies."

The expression on Ethan's face revealed his disappointment.

As far as Dana knew, he'd not done many activities outside of work and church, and she wondered if he might feel homesick or even lonely. "Why don't you come with us—if you don't mind spending the day with little kids."

He brightened. "Just let me know what time I need to show up."

"I'll give you a call later this week." Dana noticed Kim standing behind the counter and realized she needed to check in with the manager to let her know how the product testing had gone over with the customers. "See you at church tonight." She waved good-bye to Ethan.

As soon as Ethan left, Kim came out from behind the counter. "I loved those scones. How are customers liking them?"

"They're wild about them," Dana admitted. "I think we'll be able to get them behind the counter sometime next week."

"Wow, that's fast," said Kim.

Dana nodded. "We don't have much time to waste. We need to get this company back on track as quickly as possible."

Kim took a seat at an empty table and gestured for Dana to sit as well. "It looks like things are kind of serious with you and the chef."

Dana chuckled softly. "I thought you wanted to talk business."

Kim arched her eyebrows. "Well, he is a fellow employee. I had a meeting with Mr. Grady the other day, and he talked about you and Ethan constantly. He told me that Ethan goes to your church now."

"He needed a church to attend while he's here," Dana explained. "Don't get carried away, okay?"

Kim pushed out her lower lip and frowned in an exaggerated fashion. "Now I know you're not telling me something, Dana. Ever since he got here, we never talk anymore."

"Hey, I have a job to do," Dana said in defense. "I don't have much time for chitchat lately. I thought the greater issue here was to keep the bakeries in business."

Kim gave her a penetrating look. "Fine, Dana. I won't pry."

Dana sighed. "Okay, Kim. Ethan and I have been spending some time together. You could call it dating, but I don't want it to get blown out of proportion. He's only been here a month, and as far as I know, he'll be leaving as soon as he's done with his job."

Kim looked puzzled. "So, you're saying you're dating, but it's not serious?"

"We're not sure. We're praying about it. We just don't want to force a relationship that we know will have to end. If the Lord wants us to continue the relationship, He'll make a way for us. Other than that, we're basically just getting to know each other."

"Do you think you know each other pretty well?" Kim wanted to know. "I mean, like, little things. His favorite color? His mother's name? His favorite time of year?"

Dana shook her head. "I am not about to answer your pop quiz questions."

Kim wiggled her eyebrows comically. "Why not? Are you telling me you think he's perfect?"

Dana giggled. "I never said Ethan is the perfect man. We've had our share of disagreements, but I do enjoy spending time with him."

Kim laughed. "I do enjoy spending time with him," she mimicked in a high-pitched voice. "Forget the quiz. I can tell you like him, Dana. So does this mean you've given up that silly list of requirements?"

Dana put her finger to her lips and made a shushing noise. "Why do you have to bring up the list? I don't even know where I put it."

"Yeah, right. Like you don't have it memorized. I'm just glad you came to your senses. No man is ever going to meet all of those requirements, unless you hire an *actor* to be your husband."

"Yeah, I know," said Dana. "Even though Ethan's not perfect, I don't feel like I'm missing out on anything I put on the list. And I figure most men probably feel the same way."

"What do you mean?"

"I'm saying, I know my brothers have an ideal woman they'd like to end up with, but the ones who've already gotten married say that their wives have qualities they never even thought about."

Kim gave her an incredulous look. "Your brothers had lists?"

Dana shook her head. "Not exactly, but they had a general idea of what their perfect wife would be like. Now that they're married, they say the wives God gave them were better than any woman they could have imagined."

Kim nodded, a serious expression on her face. "I think your brothers may be right. I know that I've prayed about different things with a certain result in mind, and when the Lord answered my prayer, I didn't get exactly what I wanted. So many times, the result ended up better than what I had originally asked for."

"Same goes for me," Dana added. "I think what we sometimes forget is that God really is our Father, and He knows what's best for us even better than do our physical parents. Remember when we were little, and we would ask for things and our parents would give us what we *needed* instead of what we *wanted*?"

Kim nodded. "I hated that. Like getting me three pairs of reasonably-priced jeans instead on one pair of really expensive ones. My mom did stuff like that all of the time, and it drove me nuts. But she really taught me a lot about budgeting. In the long run, it made me more responsible."

"I think that's what I'm learning about my 'list,' " said Dana

"I may have something in mind, but I'm willing to let God work out all the details. I know I'll be happy with the man He wants me to marry. I've just had to learn to trust Him."

Kim agreed. "Yeah, I know it seems hard to give up your ideals, but really, we have to accept that God will make the right choice. Parents want their kids to be happy, and God feels that same way about us.

"There may be times when we experience discomfort, but He has a perfect plan. Remember when our parents took us to get shots to keep us from getting sick? The shots weren't exactly a picnic, but they protected us in the long run."

Dana nodded thoughtfully as several customers came inside the building. Kim stood up and looked toward the growing line. "I guess that means my break is over. We're a little under-staffed today, so I need to help out."

Dana smiled. "Thanks for the talk. I needed a few minutes to just chat with a girlfriend."

"No problem," said Kim. "And I know we just had that whole conversation about praying and everything but. . ." she hesitated.

"What?" asked Dana. She could tell by the glimmer in Kim's eye that her friend was in a joking mood, but she decided to play along with it.

"Just don't rush things with Ethan," said Kim. "You may think the quiz is silly, but it has some valid points."

"Like what?" Dana asked.

Kim shrugged. "I'm not sure. Personally, I would never agree to marry a man unless I knew if he liked kids. Oh, and I'd need to know his middle name."

"Why those two things?"

Kim laughed. "I don't know. Probably because I love kids and want to have at least seven and because I hate my middle name."

Dana thought for a moment. "You know, I don't think you've ever told me your middle name. What is it?"

Kim shook her head. "No way. I hate it, and I'm never telling anyone."

Dana laughed. "What if the man you want to marry just has to know before he proposes?"

Kim cocked one eyebrow. "We'll have to see about that." She turned to walk away, then stopped. Over her shoulder, she remarked, "You know how we talked about our parents wanting the best for us?"

"Yeah."

Kim shook her head and wrinkled her nose. "I think middle names are one of those things that they seem to mess up on more than other things. Maybe we should outlaw them altogether."

Dana laughed. "Oh, Kim, it can't be that bad."

Kim pursed her lips and nodded. "Oh, yes, it can. See you later."

Dana waved good-bye. "Okay. We'll be here Monday with some new bagels."

"Can't wait to taste them," said Kim. "And I'm glad you came up with this idea for the surveys. Mr. Grady is so pleased that the menu won't be set in stone until after the surveys are done."

Dana blinked in surprise. "Actually, Ethan came up with the idea. I'm just doing the organizational part of it."

Kim gave her a look that suggested she didn't believe her. "Dana, you don't have to let him take all of the credit because you like him. Mr. Grady told me you developed the plan."

Dana shook her head. "It's not all mine. It's a joint idea."

Kim shrugged. "Never mind. I guess it's not a big deal as long as it gets done."

"Right," Dana agreed. "See you later."

As Dana drove home, she thought about her list once again. Kim was right. The list didn't matter as long as God did the choosing.

Once she got home, she planned to do a massive search for that list, and if she found it, she would burn it. The time had arrived for her to take a back seat in the search process and let God be in charge.

略

Ethan watched as the basketball swished right through the hoop.

Anthony laughed and patted him on the shoulder. "That's another win for me and Ethan."

Ethan laughed as Albert and Jackson immediately began negotiating a rematch. He and Dana's brothers had spent the better part of the morning playing two-on-two at the indoor court at the gym, and Albert and Jackson had lost five of the six games they'd played.

Ethan held up his hands in surrender. "I think I'm played out for now. I'm out of shape from standing around in the kitchen all day. I need to get to the gym a little more."

Jackson scoffed, "You don't have to brag that you're out of shape when you've beaten the socks off of us."

Anthony dribbled the ball. "He's right. If I weren't on his team, he'd have lost too. I could beat the three of you by myself."

Albert and Jackson spent several moments grumbling about Anthony's boasting.

"Yeah, right," said Jackson. "We'll see who's the best when it's warm enough to play golf. Anybody can put this big ball into a basket."

"Yeah, anybody but you," quipped Anthony. "Golf? Bring it on."

Ethan laughed. His golf skills were more developed than

his basketball game, and he looked forward to getting out on the course again. He hoped he would still be here by the time they were ready to hit the links. After having bonded with these guys, he tried hard not to think about the possibility of moving on.

"Let's get some lunch," suggested Albert.

"Yeah," agreed Ethan. "Why don't you guys come over to my place, and I'll fix something to eat?"

"Sounds good to me," said Jackson. The twins agreed and after showering, the four men headed to Ethan's condo.

Over their lunch of turkey sandwiches, Albert first brought up the topic of Dana and Ethan. "Looks like you and Dana have gotten pretty serious. Want to talk about it?"

Ethan nearly choked on the water he sipped. No, he didn't want to talk about it, but from the looks on their faces, they did. He shrugged. "Maybe."

"Does she know you're not going to be here after you finish the work for the Gradys?" asked Jackson.

"Of course she does," Ethan told them.

Anthony took a more direct approach. "So why are you dating her?"

Ethan studied the three men, his gaze moving from face to face. They were serious. He held up his hands in defense. "Look, I didn't force her to go out with me. We know there's a possibility that I will leave eventually, but we decided that we'll just pray about it. In the meantime, we don't think it'll hurt to spend time together."

"So, you're saying that if you leave, you'll still continue the relationship?" asked Jackson.

Ethan took another bite of his sandwich. "We haven't really discussed that. It could happen. Or one of us could end up relocating."

Anthony shook his head. "Dana would never move away.

She loves St. Louis. Plus, she's not the type to drop her entire life for some guy."

Albert chuckled. "Especially if he doesn't line up with the list." His brothers laughed and began eating their sandwiches again.

The list? Ethan had a feeling Dana had probably not told him about this for a reason, but his curiosity forced him to ask, "What are you talking about?"

"Nothing, Man, don't worry about it," said Anthony.

"Yeah, it's a girl thing. No big deal," added Albert.

Ethan chuckled and shook his head. "Uh-uh. You can't do that to me. I want all of the details."

The brothers stopped eating and looked at each other. Suddenly, they seemed hesitant to say anything.

"Look, we shouldn't have even mentioned it," said Jackson. He gave the twins the look of a disapproving older brother. "It's Dana's thing, and if she wants to tell you about it, she will."

Ethan pushed his plate aside, his appetite gone. "Thanks a lot. If my relationship with Dana goes wrong, I'll spend the rest of my life trying to figure out what part of the list I didn't line up with."

Jackson frowned, then seemed to take pity on him. "Okay, I'll tell you this. It's Dana's list of what the ideal guy would be like. We used to tease her about it because it was so long."

"And impossible," added Anthony. "No man could be like that, so don't worry."

"Yeah, she's probably forgotten all about it," said Albert.

"Wait a minute. Back up," Ethan said, shaking his head. "What do you mean, 'No man could be like that'?" He leaned back in his chair. "Can't you give me a hint so I can at least try?"

Albert and Anthony didn't say anything. Apparently, Jackson would make the decision.

After several moments, Jackson shook his head. "Trust me, you don't want to be like this list. For one, she wrote it a long time ago. And second, a man who acted like this would have some serious problems. Nobody would like this guy."

"What?" Ethan said, feeling even more confused.

Jackson shrugged. "I don't even know how to explain it." He tilted his head toward his brothers. "You tell him."

Anthony nodded. "Here's the deal. The other day I babysat Annitra, and she wanted me to read this book to her. It was called *Anne* something."

Albert nodded. "I've had to read those books. *Anne of Green Gables*. It seems like there's at least ten of them. They never end, and she always wants to read one of them."

Anthony nodded. "Yeah. Anyway, we get to this one part, and Anne is talking to her mother or something, and she's disappointed because her friend is getting married. It's not that she doesn't want her friend to be happy, but she thinks the guy is all wrong for her. She goes on and on about how the guy wasn't wicked or wild enough.

"So then her mother says, 'Do you want her to marry some bad guy? Or would *you* want to marry a wicked man?' She thinks about it, then says, 'Well, no. But I'd like to marry somebody who could be wicked and wouldn't.' Now," Anthony crumpled up his napkin and set it down on the table for emphasis. "What in the world does that mean?"

Albert nodded. "Women want you to be all sensitive, right? But if you're too good, you're boring."

Jackson nodded and pointed at Ethan. "But if you're not nice enough, tough luck. There's no balance. If you tried to act like that, people would think you were insane. Especially women."

"So you're saying Dana's list is like that?" Ethan asked.

Anthony leaned his head to the side and thought about it for a long time. "Sort of," he said finally. "It's just a long rambling list of things she thought would be cool. But some of them aren't really practical."

Jackson laughed. "But a lot of guys who liked her got dumped because they were too different from the list. We would ask what happened to them, and she said it just didn't work out."

"Yeah, she'd say, 'Oh. . .he's nice, but. . .' " Albert shrugged. "It didn't matter. We never saw them again."

Anthony continued. "It's like, why do women get all swoony over men who act like that in books and movies? Like that *Pride and Prejudice*. What's up with that? That Darcy guy is such a jerk for so long, but women love him." He shook his head.

"Dana loves that book," added Albert. "And so do Mom, Sheryl, and Latrice."

"My wife does too," said Jackson. "Verna drags that movie out every Christmas, and it takes forever to watch it. Man, it's long."

Ethan laughed. "Seriously? Darcy?"

"Yeah, do you know him?" Anthony said, laughing.

Ethan shrugged. "You don't even want to know how much my mom liked that book, but I've never read it or seen the movie." He looked around the table. "Do you guys want to rent it?"

They shook their heads emphatically. "You can do that on your own time," said Jackson. "Just make sure you don't have anything else to do for several hours."

The men moved on to a different subject, but they no longer had Ethan's full attention. His thoughts were about Dana's list.

Before the men left, Ethan had another question for them. "So what does Dana think of me? Did she describe me as. . .*nice?*"

Albert and Anthony exchanged a look, and Albert answered first. "Yeah, she did, but only back when she first met you."

Jackson clapped a hand on Ethan's shoulder. "A word of advice. Forget about the list. Please don't try to pretend you're Mr. Darcy. She's outgrown it."

"Are you sure?"

"Positive," said Anthony. "If not, you'd be history by now." He and his brothers laughed their way down the driveway to their cars. Ethan stood in the doorway, hoping they were right.

He knew many women had an ideal in mind for potential husbands, but being up against some mysterious checklist made him nervous. He'd been feeling pretty secure in his relationship with Dana, but for the first time in a few weeks, he felt genuinely worried.

*Lord,* he prayed. *I know this is in Your hands, but if Dana's got a list, I can't compete with fiction. Please help me to do the right thing and let You guide our relationship.*

◆

"Are you sure about this?" Ethan gave Dana an incredulous look. As he hesitated, a woman with two toddlers moved past him, through the entrance gate.

Dana laughed out loud. "Yes, I'm sure. It's just a carousel, so what are you afraid of?" Shaking her head, she handed over two tickets to the operator. Without waiting for Ethan to voice any further doubts, she took hold of his hand and pulled him through the gate.

"So what's your pick? Horse, camel, or sleigh?" she asked him.

Ethan shrugged. "I don't know. I haven't been on a carousel since I was a little kid."

Dana led the way to a sleigh that would seat both of them and sat down. Patting the seat next to her, she said, "We'll ride here the first go round to get you acclimated."

Ethan shook his head. "Hey, I'm not a baby. We don't have to ride in the sleigh. It doesn't even move."

Dana grinned. "I was hoping you'd lighten up." She pointed to a nearby white horse decorated in soft pastels. "I'll ride that one."

"Then I'll take the camel next to your cotton candy horse." His voice sounded slightly gruff, but Dana could tell he was in an amiable mood.

After all of the riders were settled, the calliope music began, and the massive carousel glided to a start. After a few revolutions, Dana asked Ethan if he enjoyed the ride so far.

He smiled. "I guess so. I'll admit, this is a pretty unusual activity. I've never even seen an indoor carousel before. How old is this?"

Dana thought for a moment. "I'm not exactly sure. If I remember correctly, it was originally built in the early 1900s. It used to be kept outdoors at a different park, but eventually they moved it here."

"This is pretty cool," Ethan said. "It moves so smoothly that it's hard to imagine it's an actual antique."

"This thing was definitely built to last," Dana agreed, gently patting the brass post that protruded from her horse's back. "Isn't it kind of interesting to think that we're touching something that other people back in the 1920s touched? The world has changed so much since then; it almost seems impossible that we have this merry-go-round in common with an earlier generation."

"That's true." Ethan looked down at his clothes. "I doubt they'd be wearing jeans and tennis shoes like we are."

Dana shook her head. "Definitely not. More like suits and dresses."

The ride coasted to an end, but when Dana got ready to leave her perch, Ethan shook his head. "I'll be right back," he said, before hurrying off to talk to the ticket seller. Moments later he returned, a mile-wide grin on his face. "Pick another seat. We're good for the next five rides."

Dana laughed. Minutes ago, Ethan had grudgingly stepped on to the carousel; now, he'd bought tickets in advance.

Dana exchanged her horse for a camel. "The next five, huh?"

"Yeah. This is actually pretty fun." Ethan clambered up and took a seat on the horse next to her camel.

"Did I ever tell you I sometimes get motion sickness?" she teased.

"No, you didn't. Maybe we should sit in the sleigh."

"I'm just teasing."

"Just to be sure, let's take the sleigh this time around." Ethan cupped her waist and pulled her down, then gestured for her to step into the sleigh first. Settling in next to her, he added, "This seat doesn't go up and down like the others."

Dana giggled. "Okay, we're sitting where you want to. But, just for the record, I don't get motion sickness. I would have been fine on the camel."

As the music began and the carousel cruised to a start, Ethan reached for Dana's hand and held it. He winked. "And just for the record, I know that. I just thought it would be more romantic if we sat here together."

Dana felt her stomach flutter and took a deep breath to steady her emotions. Ethan might be stubborn about business, but he definitely had a soft side when it came to relationships—especially theirs. The way he'd looked at her made her heart melt. She'd never dated anyone else who really seemed to make such an effort to do the things she enjoyed, like riding this carousel. Ethan seemed to understand when things really mattered to her and gave his best effort to enjoy them as well.

Dana wondered to what extent she should continue to guard

her emotions from any possible hurt. Glancing sideways at Ethan, Dana realized she could do little about that now. She'd already fallen in love with him—for better, or for worse.

If he were to propose to her at this very moment, she had a feeling she'd accept without hesitation and think things through later. Given their sometimes rocky interactions at work and the fact that he still planned to continue his freelance business around the country, she wondered if she'd been too careless with her emotions. Did he feel the same way? Did he have any doubts about ending their relationship as soon as he completed his contract with the company?

Dana stole another glance at his profile. Ethan was too busy examining the architecture of the carousel to look at her, but he gave her hand a little squeeze, almost as if he knew she needed reassuring.

With a small sigh, Dana gently leaned her head on Ethan's shoulder. By now, his scent was familiar and comfortable—an unusual blend of earthy cologne and bread dough. Feeling content, Dana closed her eyes long enough for a silent prayer.

*Lord. . .I think I know what it feels like to have found the person I'm supposed to spend the rest of my life with. For that, I'm really thankful and honored that he's turning out to be so special. Even though there are a lot of things that seem overwhelming about making this relationship permanent, I'm trusting You to help us work out the details.*

ॐ

Ethan drummed the steering wheel, humming softly to himself. Normally, he hated being stuck at this particular stoplight, but today the wait at the intersection of Whispering Pines and Olive didn't feel long at all. A glance in the rearview mirror confirmed what he already knew—he practically grinned from ear to ear.

The light changed again, only allowing a few more cars to

escape the growing line of traffic. Ethan inched his car forward, still content to wait. As he glanced at the small business card on the dashboard, he wondered if this most recent chain of events had simply been a coincidence.

The night before, he'd stopped to chat with his landlord. Dave occupied the condo next to Ethan's. During the course of their conversation, Ethan had jokingly mentioned that he'd been considering opening his future restaurant in the St. Louis area.

Without hesitation, his landlord had suggested Ethan get in touch with his cousin, who just happened to be a real estate agent specializing in commercial properties. "Shari might have something she can show you," Dave said enthusiastically.

Ethan nodded agreeably but didn't give the idea of going much thought. Half an hour later, Dave phoned to inform Ethan that not only did Shari have a property listed that he might want to see, but she could show it the next morning.

Ethan tentatively scheduled an appointment yet did some intense prayer that night. In the morning, he awakened feeling confident that he wanted to keep the appointment.

After calling work to let Mr. Grady know he'd be a bit late, he rushed off to make his appointment with Shari. She'd ultimately shown him half a dozen different properties that could easily meet his list of requirements.

In the past, he'd always assumed that he'd have to build his own restaurant, but now he felt a surge of excitement. Purchasing an existing building would put him that much closer to his goal.

The light changed once more, finally allowing Ethan to get back in motion. Continuing toward work, he again pondered the idea of remaining in St. Louis. The notion to stay here had crossed his mind more than a few times, especially now that he and Dana were so close.

He'd always envisioned starting his business somewhere closer to New York, but he knew Dana loved her hometown as well. Might there be some room for a compromise? If so, who would be the one to relocate?

Even though he'd just looked at potential buildings to house his restaurant, Ethan didn't feel one hundred percent sure that St. Louis was his ideal location.

He thought back to the previous week when he and Dana had ridden the carousel at Faust Park. Six months ago, he'd have had a hard time imagining himself on a merry-go-round nine times nonstop. After the first few times, the motion had become a little monotonous, but he didn't care. Watching the pleasure on Dana's face and being able to hold her hand for so long had been worth the wave of dizziness he felt when he set foot on solid ground after the ride ended.

The truth was obvious. He loved Dana, even though he couldn't pinpoint the exact moment he lost his heart to her. At some point in time, attraction had become admiration, which in turn developed into respect. Respect had expanded to include friendship, and without his giving much thought to the progression of friendship, Ethan had been led to the brink of falling in love.

"So now what?" Ethan asked himself aloud. Returning to New York would be difficult, but he missed his home, family, and friends. Though there was a chance Dana might want to leave St. Louis, he had a feeling such a drastic move would not meet with a favorable reception from her family.

The last thing he wanted to do was try to convert their relationship into a phone and E-mail romance. But were they close enough to move beyond simply dating one another? Had the time come for a deeper commitment?

Ethan slowed his car to a stop at yet another light. Shaking his head, he contemplated his choices. No matter how much he avoided the facts, his time in St. Louis rapidly drew to a close. He could either propose to Dana and see what happened or go back to New York and try to continue the relationship as best he could.

Ethan drummed his fingers on the steering wheel again and waited for the light to change.

Too much had happened in the past twenty-four hours for him to make a coherent decision. He needed to be sure that when he made a choice, he made the right one.

"I don't want to mess this up," he rationalized. After several more moments of consideration, Ethan decided to take an entire week to devote some serious prayer time to his concerns.

"Lord, I know I've asked You to show me Your will before, but if I ever needed to make the right choice about something, now is definitely the time."

As soon as the words left his mouth, a feeling of contentment washed over Ethan, giving him the reassurance he so needed. There was no mistaking that sense of peace. As long as he didn't put his own feelings over God's plan, he knew he was definitely on the right track.

# *ten*

"Hmm. . .What's the special occasion?" Dana asked. Ethan stood in the doorway of her office, holding a bagel with cream cheese smeared on top. He had jabbed two small candles into the top, and as the flames danced, melted wax slid down into the cream cheese. Ethan held the bagel out to her, but Dana shook her head. "I'll pass. I'm not into eating wax."

"At least blow out the candles."

Dana quickly blew and returned her attention to the inventory sheets she'd been studying.

Ethan cut the bagel in half. "You sure you don't want a piece? It's pumpernickel."

Dana wrinkled her nose. "How many times do I have to tell you, I can't stand pumpernickel?"

He shrugged. "It seems weird that two people so perfect for each other can be so different. I still can't believe you don't like pumpernickel."

She shrugged. "Well, I don't. And a couple can hardly find out if they're perfect for each other in a few weeks."

"Eight weeks," said Ethan. "That's the special occasion. Today is the two month anniversary of the day I got here."

Dana glanced at the calendar on her wall. "Wow, I didn't even realize it. Time is moving so fast."

Ethan cleared his throat. "I know. I wanted to ask you something."

Dana nodded and forced herself to remain calm. Lately, the question of whether or not Ethan would return to New York had been weighing heavily on their minds. She knew more than ever that she didn't want him to leave, but Ethan had to make the final choice. If he felt the Lord wanted him to return home, she couldn't argue with that.

She gave Ethan her bravest smile and waited for him to say what he'd come to say.

"I love you," he said simply. "I know two months shouldn't be enough time to fall in love, but that's what happened." He reached for her hands and held them in his. Looking into her eyes, he continued. "I'd feel pretty relieved if I knew how you felt about me."

Dana laughed, still trying to appear calm. Inside, her stomach turned somersaults as her brain replayed Ethan's sentence over and over again.

*I love you.* Those were the words she'd been waiting to hear. Of course she loved him too. As much as she'd prayed for guidance, she felt at peace. Surely, this was God's will.

Ethan had confirmed what she'd been feeling, and she couldn't ever remember being happier. Without a second thought, she reached forward and hugged him. "I love you too."

Ethan pulled away from her. "Are you sure about that? I don't have a test to pass or anything? I don't have to give up pumpernickel bagels?"

Dana shook her head. "I'm sure." As she looked at him, she knew this was what it felt like when prayers were answered. Everything fell into place perfectly, and there were no rough spots. The Lord's fingerprints were all over this.

"I think this means I also have an answer about moving back to New York," Ethan told her. "I've been praying about it, and I really think I want to open my restaurant here."

Dana felt so happy, she could hardly speak. She'd been praying about this as well, and she never felt the Lord leading her to leave St. Louis. Knowing Ethan wanted to move here was a great comfort. "That sounds wonderful."

"Of course, I'll have to do some hard bargaining with Mr. Grady so I can hire you to work for me," he laughed. "And don't worry, I won't be bossy. It'll be a real partnership, husband and wife working side by side. I'll let you do your thing with the business side, and I'll be in charge of cooking."

Dana hesitated. His sudden talk of marriage caught her off guard. Of course, she had expected nothing less than a marriage proposal, but he had merely jumped from "I love you" to "husband and wife." Though they were in love, she hadn't expected a proposal from him this soon.

In Ethan's mind, she had quit her job, married him, and agreed to manage his restaurant.

Ethan must have noticed the look on her face. "Hey, what's wrong? I thought you'd be happy."

Dana swallowed as she tried to think of how to explain how she felt. "I'm fine. It just seems like everything's moving so fast without much warning."

"I know, I know—but we don't have to approach this at the speed of light. I just thought we'd need to make sure we feel the same."

Ripples of relief melted over Dana. "I agree. And I think we should still keep praying about this—just to be sure," she explained. "I mean, it's way too early to think about marriage. We still don't know each other that well."

Ethan folded his arms. "What do you mean? I think we know each other pretty well."

Dana struggled to find the words to answer him. At a loss for an explanation, she fell back on Kim's reasoning. "What's my favorite color?"

"Yellow," Ethan said, not missing a beat.

"My favorite time of year?"

Ethan grinned. "Winter. You love snow as long as you don't

have to drive in it."

"My middle name?"

"Marie." He leaned forward and spoke in a mock whisper. "So do I pass the test?"

"It's not a test. . ." Dana said. She had to admit he had learned a lot about her. Likewise, she knew he loved spring, the color green, and his middle name was. . .Okay, she didn't know his middle name yet. Dana could see room for improvement.

She tilted her head to the side, thinking. Finally, she said, "We still need to get to know each other better. I don't know your middle name yet. What is it?"

Ethan shrugged. "You're kidding, right? The last time I checked, middle names weren't the magic word to get to the altar. In fact, I thought I just needed to say, 'Will you marry me?'"

Dana sat very still for a moment. "Are you asking me to marry you?"

"Not quite," said Ethan.

So what did he mean? "Then what are you saying?"

Ethan stood up. "I'm saying I *will* ask you to marry me soon, but I'm not so unromantic that I'm going to ask you while we're at work, and you're sitting at your desk surrounded by a million papers."

Dana laughed. He had artfully avoided her middle name question, but she didn't mind letting her almost-fiancé off the hook for now. Maybe, like Kim, he hated his middle name. "Thank you for the warning."

"You're welcome," said Ethan. "I hate to cut this visit short, but I need to get back to the kitchen and check on my banana muffins."

Dana lifted an eyebrow. "You're making plain banana muffins? That's a first."

"Actually. . .they're banana pineapple with chocolate chunks and coconut. Sort of tropical with chocolate thrown in for the fun of it."

Dana's stomach growled at that instant. Had dinnertime come so soon? "I may be down to have a sample later on."

"You'd better hurry," he warned. "Everyone wants to taste these, and I might not have any left if you wait too long."

"I'll do my best. I've still got the surveys from yesterday to look over."

"Oh, right. Let me know how the bread pudding went over. If it's still not working, I have another idea. I'll see you later." Just before he left, he blew her a kiss.

Dana caught it and blew one to him in return. Her first kiss from Ethan just happened to be one that didn't feel like anything. At least, the feeling wasn't *tangible*—but if she could bottle the emotional high that accompanied the airborne kiss, she'd be a millionaire. She could see it now, lined up neatly on shelves at major department stores, in fancy bottles. *Airborne Kiss, by Dana,* the bottle would read. She would become rich and famous.

Dana laughed aloud at the idea. "For one thing, it wouldn't be sitting on the shelves. It would be flying out the door," she said, grinning. Being in love was fantabulous.

As Dana considered this feeling, her gaze landed on a stack of recent surveys, and a deep sigh escaped her lips.

While being in love felt amazing, telling Ethan he would have to cut one of his recipes from the menu would be the total opposite. The challenge lay in finding a way to break the news gently. The way she felt right now, she would rather ignore the problem, but in her heart, she knew it must be done.

The majority of the recipes had done well with the customers. Although some of the recipes had needed some extensive adjustments, Dana had been forced to eat her words a number of times. At least, until Ethan invented the bread pudding.

The pumpernickel-walnut-cherry bread pudding, to be exact. The first time they'd offered it to people, the majority of customers had agreed that it just wasn't something they would buy.

Ethan had persisted, feeling confident that he could tweak the recipe to make it more appealing. He'd returned to the test kitchen and emerged with virtually the same dish, with the addition of ginger and caramel.

She and Ethan had returned to the stores and asked people to taste it again. This time, people had been a tad more reluctant. Again, to Ethan's dismay, the response had not been good.

Instead of giving up, Ethan went back to the kitchen and returned with a brand new dish that Dana had considered to be more of a monstrosity than a dessert. The already overly flavored pudding now boasted coconuts, raisins, lime zest, and dried cranberries.

"Have you even tasted this?" Dana asked Ethan.

He became instantly offended and barely spoke as they conducted the surveys. By this time, most people tried to pretend they didn't see the sample table. They practically had to beg people to come and taste it, and as Dana had expected, the response turned out to be far from favorable.

Dana took a look at one of the most recent questionnaires.

*I can't imagine why you would put so many flavors in a dessert. I can't even tell what this tastes like*, one sampler had written.

Another wrote, *What is this supposed to be? Surely not bread pudding?*

The others were pretty much the same, ranging from eloquent and tactful: *This is not really something I'd like to serve to guests. I think dessert should be a time for simplicity instead of another excuse to overload the taste buds,* to simple: *It tastes terrible! Sorry. . . .*

Poor Ethan. He was obviously proud of this recipe and wanted very much for it to remain on the menu. In Dana's opinion, and according to their agreement, it had to be cut. No one seemed interested in eating or buying it, and with the amount of ingredients it called for, it would be a major waste of the bakers' time and the company's money.

Dana leaned back in her chair and tried to determine how in the world she would break the news to him. He really seemed attached to whatever he created, and when faced with criticism, he sometimes took it as a personal insult.

She decided not to think about it right now. She would let a few days pass and see if he focused his interest on a different recipe. Maybe by then he would be more willing to let go of that awful bread pudding.

❧

"Hi there," said Ethan, as he entered Dana's office. "I got your voice mail. What did you need to talk about?"

An unreadable look crossed over her face. "Could you sit down for a minute?"

Ethan sat down, trying to fight the apprehension that settled over him. Pasting a smile he didn't feel on his face, he asked, "Anything wrong?"

Dana spoke quietly. "Actually, yes. Remember our agreement about the recipes and the survey?"

Ethan nodded. "Yeah."

"Okay. I think it's time to get rid of the pumpernickel bread pudding."

Ethan laughed, feeling relieved. "You're joking, right? You're just kidding because you hate pumpernickel." Dana didn't answer. "Right?" Ethan prodded.

Dana gave him an apologetic look. "I'm sorry, but I'm really not kidding." She shook her head. "We just can't put it on the menu."

"Hey, wait a minute," he argued. "We agreed that I could tweak things to make it better, remember?"

Dana shook her head. "You've tweaked twice, and now people are practically running from it. With all of the ingredients you have in it, I'm not surprised. It bears a striking resemblance to fruitcake."

Ethan winced. He realized it hadn't exactly gotten rave reviews, but he refused to believe it had been that terrible.

Dana continued. "We just can't keep wasting time and money on it."

Ethan tugged at his collar. Had Dana done this just to prove that people wouldn't like all of his recipes? So far, the response for everything else had been good, and he felt confident he could fix the bread pudding. "Give me another chance."

Dana shook her head. "Look, Ethan, Mr. Grady is wanting to get this menu in place. We still have to test your new muffins and those croissants. Let's just cut our losses on the pudding, okay?"

"I don't think so. People might not recognize it, but that dish is a gourmet masterpiece. It might not take off right now, but give it a few months."

Dana sighed. "Ethan, please don't make this harder. I know I've been really supportive about your changing the other recipes. We both know I didn't think many of them would work. Do you think it felt good to eat my words time and time again?"

Ethan didn't answer. This was his favorite recipe, and he couldn't believe she had decided to be so unreasonable.

Dana spoke up again. "Plus, it has a million ingredients and will cost a fortune to make. It'll just get moldy sitting there and never being sold."

At that moment, Mr. Grady came into the office, waving a glossy magazine. "Look! Grady Bakeries is mentioned in this month's issue of *Restaurant Owner.*"

"Wow," said Dana. "I hope they said good things."

Mr. Grady grinned. "You bet. And it's all because of Ethan." He whipped his reading glasses out of his pocket, put them on, and began to read.

*"Chef Ethan D. Miles, culinary genius and knight in shining armor for countless numbers of failing restaurants, has left New York to focus on the Heartland for the time being. Miles is applying his know-how to making over the menu at the St. Louis-based Grady Bakeries.*

*"If his previous record is any indication of how he'll fare, Grady Bakeries will be back on track immediately. It's still anyone's guess as to when Chef Miles will settle down and apply his creativity to his own restaurant. Until then, stop by one of the Grady Bakeries to get a taste of his latest ingenuity."*

Mr. Grady closed the magazine emphatically. "This is excellent. I've dreamed about getting a mention in this magazine. This is an answer to prayer."

"That's excellent," Dana agreed. "Ethan, you really do know what you're doing."

The glowing review pleased Ethan. He'd heard a great many compliments concerning his work, but this had come at a time when he really needed the encouragement. Turning to Dana, he said, "Now will you let me keep the bread pudding on the menu?"

Dana's jaw dropped. "We had an agreement. You promised."

Mr. Grady interrupted. "What's this about bread pudding?"

Dana shot Ethan a glare, and he didn't say anything. He hadn't expected Mr. Grady to get into the disagreement.

"Mr. Grady," Dana began, "Ethan and I agreed when we decided to do the surveys that if anything just didn't seem to work with the customers, we would get rid of it."

"But we also agreed that I could work with the recipe for awhile," Ethan added.

"For how long?" argued Dana. "All you've done is add things to it."

Mr. Grady frowned. "Dana, I think the least we can do is let Ethan work with it. Even if the pudding doesn't sell immediately, word may get around that Ethan's created the recipe, and that might boost sales."

Dana was incredulous. "Do you really think putting Ethan's name on that thing will pick up sales?"

Sighing, Mr. Grady said, "In times like this, every little bit helps."

"That's my point, exactly," said Dana. "Every bit does count, and this recipe is too expensive to make. It has a thousand ingredients and won't be cost effective unless we charge an exorbitant amount per serving, and people buy it right and left. As of now, people don't even want to taste a free sample."

Ethan realized Dana did have a point, but since Mr. Grady seemed to be on his side, he didn't want to look a gift horse in the mouth. He had complete confidence he could fix this recipe.

"Dana," Ethan said, trying to think of a way to calm her down. "When I came up with the plan to do the surveys, I only wanted to help you feel better. You didn't think people would like my ideas, so I tried to think of a way to make the menu more comfortable for you—but I still have the final say in this."

"You thought of the survey?" asked Mr. Grady. "I thought that was Dana's idea."

Dana shook her head. "No. Ethan came up with it, and I did the organizing."

Crossing his arms, Mr. Grady frowned deeply. "Dana, I'm disappointed. All along I've been thinking you came up with the concept, and I was proud of Ethan for agreeing to it." He shook his head. "But this is appalling. You're telling me that Ethan, who's done this job time and time again came up with the idea to appease you? I remember how you complained that no one would buy his recipes, but I thought you'd gotten over it."

Ethan had never heard Mr. Grady like this before. He actually sounded angry. Dana looked absolutely flabbergasted, and Ethan wanted to jump in and smooth things out, but he didn't. If he let Dana have her way now, the bread pudding would be permanently shelved.

"Mr. Grady, please let me explain—" said Dana.

Mr. Grady pursed his lips and shook his head. "I'm afraid it's not up for discussion, Dana. I'm the one who has the final say, and I want that bread pudding in the stores along with everything else he's created for us."

Tears welled up in Dana's eyes. Ethan felt like his heart had been torn in two. Should he pick Dana over the bread pudding?

She nodded slowly. "I see." She opened her desk and began pulling out several items.

"What are you doing? Ethan asked.

Dana looked at Mr. Grady. "I'm sorry, but as the overseeing manager of Grady Bakeries, I can't stand by and watch this man waste your money over something so ridiculous. If you want to know how people feel about that pudding, take a look at these survey sheets." She gestured toward a stack of papers. "I have forced myself to be humble when I'm wrong, but he refuses to admit defeat on a bread pudding." Juggling the armload of items she'd removed from her desk, she reached for her purse.

"Please accept my resignation, effective immediately. If Ethan knows my job so well, I suggest that he take my place." Without another word, she sailed through the doorway and disappeared into the hallway.

Ethan was too stunned to talk.

Apparently, Mr. Grady felt the same way. Mr. Grady didn't

say a word, but after several moments, he jammed his hands into his pockets and left the office.

Ethan remained in the room alone, feeling like he had been hit in the chest with a rock. What had he done? Was Dana only upset about work, or would this disagreement spill over into their personal relationship? Had he just allowed his ego to ruin the chance to spend the rest of his life with the woman he loved?

❧

*Stay calm,* Dana told herself as she walked to her car. She unlocked the door and got inside after tossing her belongings on the passenger's seat.

Before she started the car, she took several moments to take deep breaths, in hopes of subduing her emotions.

*Did I really just quit my job?*

She wanted to cry. Dana had poured her heart and soul into that job, and she walked away from it. She needed to find a new job and house, since the Gradys owned the small house she now rented. But Ethan's attitude upset her the most. Talk about prideful! The way his nose tilted in the air, he would drown if it rained.

Pumpernickel bread pudding indeed! What would it take for him to admit that it hadn't been appetizing in the least?

With a groan, Dana started the engine. In all likelihood, men would walk on Mars before Ethan admitted defeat.

Looking toward the building, another thought occurred to her. If Ethan really cared about anyone's feelings other than his own, he would have come after her by now. Obviously, he was too far gone to change. And she didn't know what to think about Mr. Grady's behavior. Apparently, he had sold her out for a magazine article.

Dana tuned the radio to the classical music station as she drove. She wished the sound of the music would erase the pain she felt. Her relationship with the man she loved—or, at least, thought she loved was over. It looked like Ethan wasn't Prince Charming after all.

≈

The phone rang, jolting Dana out of her sleep. "Hello?" she asked groggily.

The person on the other end sighed. "Dana, it's me."

"Yes, Ethan?" She held back the emotional stream of questions she wanted to ask him.

"It's nine-thirty, and you're not in the office. I need to know what's going on with you."

Dana cleared her throat. Of all the nerve. . . "In case you weren't paying attention, *Chef* Miles, I resigned yesterday. Therefore, I have no need to be at work today."

"Dana, come on. Don't be childish about this—"

"I'm not the one being childish," Dana cut him off. "You're the one who can't admit your recipe stinks. It's only one measly recipe, so what difference does it make?"

He hesitated, and Dana tried to imagine the look on his face. Was it at all possible that he felt torn between her and his precious bread pudding?

"Dana, really, the Gradys need you here. Mr. Grady is in utter shock, and everyone is speculating about what's happened. Please come back."

Tears rolled down Dana's cheeks. She hated the fact that she had walked out on her job. That type of action wasn't typical of her at all. She felt terrible about leaving the Gradys at a time when they were so vulnerable—but that hadn't stopped Ethan from taking advantage of a struggling company.

"I can't. Really." Wasting no time, she hung up the phone before Ethan could reply. Dana cried herself to sleep again. Ethan still hadn't mentioned their relationship. Did that mean it had ended? Would he change his mind and go back to New York now?

❧

Ethan gave up on calling after a couple of days. After explaining the situation to Albert and Anthony, they assured him that he should just let Dana have some time alone instead of continuing his hourly pleas for her to come back to work.

"By Sunday, she'll be in a better mood," Anthony assured him. "Come to dinner at Mom and Dad's, and you can talk to her then."

"I don't know if that's such a good idea," Ethan hedged. "I seriously doubt she'll invite me."

"Then I'm inviting you." Anthony's tone let Ethan know he saw no problem with the idea. "You need to talk to each other, and if she won't pick up the phone, you can find a way to have a conversation then."

Ethan continued his quest to get Dana to return his calls, but it didn't work. Instead, he poured out his heart to the answering machine, but to no avail.

He tried going to her house, but she wouldn't answer the door. By the end of the week, she had left her house to spend a few days with her parents, according to Anthony.

At work, things headed toward shambles. The survey system ground to a standstill because Dana had been the one in charge of running it. Orders, inventory sheets, and requisitions constantly came in from the three stores. Mr. Grady, along with the rest of the staff, was doing his best to divide Dana's duties. To put things simply, no one realized how much she had done until she wasn't there to do it any longer.

Mr. Grady tried calling her, but he met with the answering machine as well.

At church, she avoided Ethan like the flu. When he sat next to her on the pew, she didn't even turn to look at him. That had really stung.

Still, Ethan wanted to attend dinner at her parents' in hopes of trying to speak to her.

After checking with Anthony to see if the invitation still stood, Ethan steeled himself and decided to go. Hopefully, Dana would respond better if they were face-to-face. At least it was worth a try. The worst that could happen would be that she would just choose not to talk to him.

At Mavis and Claude's, Ethan patiently waited for the right moment. First, she disappeared into the kitchen to help with the meal. Afterwards, she washed dishes, then played with her young nieces and nephews. Finally, when she went to the kitchen to cut one of the neighbors a piece of Mavis's butter cake, Ethan saw his chance and jumped at it.

He followed her into the kitchen, then started his speech. "Dana, please come back to work. We need you there. Mr. Grady is so embarrassed that he yelled at you. He didn't mean it, and he wants you back. I want you there. So does everyone else."

Dana didn't look up from the cake she was cutting. "So what's going on with the new recipes? Are they in the stores yet?"

"Not yet. We've hit a few snags, since you were the one coordinating all of that."

Dana pursed her lips. "And the bread pudding?"

Ethan didn't answer. She had made this too personal. Now he owed it to himself to get that recipe figured out.

Dana sighed and picked up the saucer. "It looks like you all are handling things just fine without me."

Ethan touched her arm to keep her from running away. "You know that's not true. Don't do this."

Dana shook her head. "I have an interview tomorrow morning at The Loaf. It's a little trendy for my taste, and I won't be district manager, but I think I'll get the job." Her eyes took on a hurt look. "I'd rather not talk about this again. I'm really trying to put it all behind me."

Ethan nodded. She had made up her mind, and arguing about it would do no good. "What about us?" he asked hopefully. "We were about to get engaged."

Pain danced across Dana's face. She bit her lip, then looked at the floor. "I don't know. I need some time to pray."

She eased away from him and headed back to the living room. She might as well have just said, "It's over." Feeling crushed, Ethan quietly retrieved his coat and gloves and left. He couldn't stand being in the house with her if she wouldn't talk to him.

               *৯*

Dana sat in the parking lot outside The Loaf's regional office. She had aced the interview and would start Monday as the manager of one of the suburban stores in Chesterfield—but did she really want to take this final step away from all she'd worked for at Grady's?

She didn't know. Instead of trying to decide, she took a drive. As though her car were on automatic pilot, she ended up in the Grady headquarters parking lot. From the exterior, everything looked the same as it had been when she'd left. She wondered if things inside were still favorable.

Had Ethan been exaggerating when he'd said they were willing to take her back?

Dana leaned her forehead against the steering wheel and prayed. "Lord, I don't want to go back in there, but I gave the Gradys my word that I would do my best for them. I don't feel right about leaving now, but I don't feel thrilled with the idea of working with Ethan either.

"He's so wasteful and arrogant, Lord. Even though I love him, I don't know if we could really ever be happy together. He has to have his way, even when someone might get hurt.

"I miss him, but he really confused me last week when he stood there and said nothing about his part. Meanwhile, he shut his mouth while Mr. Grady blamed me. I didn't mess things up, Lord. It's not my fault. I'm not the one who needs to have a better attitude. I'm not the one who has the ego problem."

*Aren't you?*

The thought was startlingly clear. Dana sat up and looked around, convinced someone had spoken the words aloud.

"Am I Lord? Is it my fault?"

*A man's pride brings him low, but a man of lowly spirit gains honor.*

The verse was Proverbs 29:23, and she had learned it in high school. Why had it popped into her mind just now?

Dana took a long look at her situation. In all honesty, she had to admit that she felt pretty low right now. Try as she might to blame Ethan, he still had his job, his house, and his dignity. She, on the other hand, had lost these things by storming out of the building in a huff.

Ethan wasn't the only one causing problems. She'd spent time focusing on his ego problems, failing to realize she had her own struggles with pride. She thought she'd overcome it when Ethan's recipes had become such a success, but she'd only been fooling herself. God knew her pride had merely lain dormant, stewing, bubbling, and waiting for a crack in the surface.

Dana had felt bad for Ethan concerning his bread pudding, but the sense of vindication had quickly overtaken any genuine sadness. She had been happy to see Ethan fail for once. She couldn't wait to hear him admit that he'd been wrong. All along, *she'd* been wrong. What difference did it make to her if he never apologized or admitted his attitude had been bad?

She wasn't his judge. The only One who deserved to hear apologies from any human being was God, the creator of earth and everything on its face and within its depths.

Dana leaned forward again and sobbed. "Oh, God, please

forgive me. I've been doing this all wrong. I am not Your instrument to exact correct behavior from other people. Help me to mind my own business, Lord."

Dana remembered one of her mother's favorite phrases. "If everybody really minded his own business, the world would be a much quieter place. We wouldn't have time to do anything else. As far as God is concerned, we have enough personal business to keep us occupied from the day we get here until the day we leave this earth."

Dana never paid attention to this statement before, but now she saw just how accurate her mother had been.

Suddenly, she knew exactly what she needed to do. She would apologize to Mr. Grady and Ethan and get her job back. She'd given her word and wasn't about to go back on it.

Her dignity stung at the thought of the task ahead, but Dana ignored the feeling. It had already gotten her in more than enough trouble.

# eleven

"Coming!" Dana ran downstairs to answer the doorbell. She hadn't been expecting any company and was pleasantly surprised to see her mother on the other side of the peephole.

"Hi, Mom." Dana reached out and gave her mom a hug and a quick peck on the cheek. Her mother carried a picnic basket on her arm, and judging from the looks of it, it was heavy. "Is everything okay?"

"It will be when I'm done." Mom headed for the kitchen without even removing her coat. "I brought you breakfast."

Dana hesitated before following. This did not seem like a good sign. The "traveling breakfast buffet," as her siblings had called it meant Mom was up to something serious. Most likely, her mother had a specific discussion in mind, and Dana wasn't so sure the topic would be an easy one.

When she reached the kitchen, Mom had pulled nearly everything imaginable from that basket. Preserves, bacon, biscuits, fruit, and lots of other little items came from the depths.

Dana's stomach did a little flip-flop. Was she in trouble? Had she done something to upset her mother? Rather than pry and run the risk of making things more difficult, Dana decided she would let Mom take the lead.

Only after they filled their plates and sat down to eat did Mom get down to business.

"You know I'm proud of you for going back to your job, don't you?"

Dana nodded. "That means a lot to me. But I needed to do it. I couldn't just leave them in the lurch."

Mom nodded. "You're a good worker, and they appreciate you. Mrs. Grady told me that just yesterday."

Dana smiled. Hearing second hand information that her bosses still liked her felt good. In fact, it was a major relief. Mr. Grady had been rather quiet after she'd returned two weeks ago. He was probably trying to figure out what had made her fly off the handle in the first place, but not knowing exactly how he felt still made Dana a little nervous.

"And how is Ethan?"

*Ah ha!* Dana held back a smile. The real reason for the breakfast buffet became clear. Her mother wanted to see how things were with Ethan.

Dana picked at her scrambled eggs, choosing her words carefully. "I guess he's doing okay. I see him at work occasionally and at church."

"Your brothers said you and Ethan have stopped dating. Is that true?"

"Basically. It's the only thing we can do right now. Besides, there's a lot going on at work. The new menu is almost in place, but it's still pretty busy around the office."

"How long has it been since you had the falling out with that boy?"

"Three weeks yesterday."

"And you don't mind having your relationship up in the air like this?" Mom prodded.

"Well, it's no picnic, but I can't force him to change. He's too arrogant for his own good and being around him so much makes me act worse. I'm really doing my best to stay away from him."

"Why?"

Dana blinked. "Because it's hard for me to separate my personal feelings from business. I want to, but it's hard."

"Last week you said you were working on your own attitude," reminded Mom. "So I guess you're back to trying to fix him, right?"

Dana winced. Her mother was right: she had slipped into old habits rather quickly. She took a deep breath. "I'll pray about it."

"Good. And maybe you should talk to Ethan."

"Not while he's still gloating about his bread pudding making it into the stores. I, for one, have checked with all three stores, and it isn't selling." Dana sighed deeply. "The whole thing is frustrating."

Mom just nodded. They finished the rest of their breakfast, then washed the dishes. Dana relaxed, realizing she was off the hook now. Her mother had made her point, and Dana didn't have to worry about what might be coming next.

At least it seemed that way. "How about a movie?" asked Mom as she put away the last of the dishes.

"Like what? There's not too much to see at the show lately."

Mom shook her head. "I meant on video. I brought my copy of *Pride and Prejudice*. Do you want to watch it with me?"

Dana didn't particularly feel like watching a movie, but she decided to please her mother. Besides, as long as the movie played, she didn't have to worry about anything else. She might even be able to relax for a few hours.

As she watched, Dana forgot her own problems and became immersed in the plot of the movie. When it ended, Dana and her mother sat on the couch and talked for awhile.

"Dana," said her mother, "I won't try to tell you what to do, but I think you're being a little hard on Ethan."

"I think he went a little hard on me. I feel so betrayed that he would jeopardize our relationship for something so trivial."

"I know, Honey, but nobody's perfect. Think about the movie we just watched. It took Elizabeth and Mr. Darcy a while to get on the same page, but eventually, they did start to understand each other. Both of them had their faults, but they did love each other."

"Mom, you really can't compare real life to a movie," Dana countered. "Besides, if Ethan really wanted to sort this out, he wouldn't be clinging to that silly bread pudding. He would try to understand how I feel."

"I don't want you to get bitter about this. That's why I'm concerned."

Dana smiled. "Thanks, Mom. I promise I won't be bitter about this. I'm trying to work on forgiving him, but for now, I need to stay away from him. Otherwise, it just hurts too much."

Mom leaned over and hugged Dana. "Honey, I'm so proud of you. I was concerned about how you were handling all of this, but I feel much better after our talk."

Dana chuckled. Her mother did sometimes have the tendency to go overboard with worry, and Dana felt glad her mother was relieved.

After another half hour of chatting, Mom left to go home.

"When you don't know what else to do, pray," her mother reminded her. "Actually, just pray—even when you think you know what to do. You can never go to the Lord too much."

"I know, Mom. I don't want you fretting about me. If the Lord wants Ethan and me to start our relationship again, He'll let us know."

After Mom left, Dana decided to get outside for a little while. Her mother was right about one thing—she'd spent far too much time closed up in the house. It was mid-March, and spring waited just around the corner.

Dana spent the rest of the day working in her yard, pulling

weeds and digging flowerbeds in preparation for planting in another month or so.

By the time she went in for the day, she was thoroughly exhausted but in good spirits.

*૨*

Dana's resolve was put to the test the following Monday. As she conducted her progress report at the store Craig managed, she was pleased and relieved to find that business had picked up.

Craig and his employees were also breathing a sigh of relief. "This menu is excellent," he told Dana as she completed her report. "It's fresh, new, and it tastes good. The customers are glad to see something different, but they're also happy that we kept some of the old favorites like the honey oatmeal and the old-fashioned raisin bread."

Dana nodded, pleased to hear that things were going well. "Any suggestions I can take back to Mr. Grady?"

Craig shrugged. "I know I shouldn't say this, but I think we need to ditch that pumpernickel bread pudding. It's a pain to keep warm, and it's just taking up space since it's not selling well."

*You don't say?* Dana thought. *Why doesn't that surprise me?*

"I could put out more cinnamon rolls in the same space and sell them all before lunch."

Dana made a note of Craig's idea and tried to remain objective. "I'll let Mr. Grady know," she said. It was all she could say to keep the lid on what she really felt about the issue.

"Thanks," Craig agreed. "If you want, I could call Mr. Grady and tell him so myself."

Dana shrugged. "You really don't have to. It's my job to report the managers' concerns back to him, so don't worry about it."

"Hey, don't get offended," Craig told her. "I just thought it might be easier for you." He paused, as if deciding if he should say more. Finally, he added, "Because, you know, there are a lot of rumors going on about you walking out on the company, and everyone's pretty much blaming that chef Mr. Grady hired. We think he's done a great job overall, but we're behind you one hundred percent on this bread pudding thing. It's a total bomb."

Dana felt quite elated that others were on her side as well. They were basing their opinions on what happened in the stores—something Mr. Grady had not yet noticed.

Still, she couldn't get too involved in this issue because she wanted to remain loyal to Mr. Grady. Furthermore, her conscience would be on red alert if she got involved in gossip.

Realizing Craig waited for her answer, Dana smiled and took a deep breath. "Thanks, Craig. Like I said, I'll give this information to Mr. Grady. I know we all have our frustrations, but the company is in a vulnerable position right now, so I think it's best if we all throw our support behind Mr. Grady so we can be united.

"Talking about things behind his back won't really do anything but create a lot of tension, so I can't share my opinion with anyone but him. It's not the easiest thing to do, but it's really best for the company. He'll be paying close attention to sales records for the next few months, so if something just isn't working, he'll notice the figures."

Craig nodded. "Hey, I understand. And I'm not trying to start any trouble or anything. I want this company to get better too."

"Good." Dana peeked back out front where the midday crowd started to pour in. "It looks like we're on the road to recovery," she told him.

28

Ethan paused outside the door to Dana's office. He could hear her on the phone, talking with one of the suppliers. Apparently, there had been a sudden spike in the price of flour, and Dana wanted to get to the bottom of the matter.

Ethan grinned. That was classic Dana, always frugal, always looking at the bottom line. But she had a soft spot for making people happy, even if it meant spending a few extra dollars here and there.

He lightly rapped on the door, deciding that it would be easier to go in there while she spoke on the phone. They hadn't had a real conversation in the three weeks since she'd come back to work, and he needed to talk to her before it was too late.

She smiled when he entered, and she seemed genuinely pleased to see him.

She held up five fingers, indicating she would be off the phone shortly. Ethan waited patiently, trying to decide exactly what he should say to her.

He had completed his assignment, and after the day ended, he would no longer be employed by Grady Bakeries. The menu was in place and doing well in the stores—for the most part. He'd done more work on the bread pudding and felt confident that it would start selling soon. Sometimes, things took time, and thankfully, Mr. Grady had offered to give the dish the extra chance that Dana had refused him.

He'd been surprised when she'd quit her job, but he'd been even more amazed that she'd actually come back to work, apologized, and picked up like nothing had ever happened.

Even more admirable was her general attitude about the ordeal. She still avoided one-on-one conversations with him, but she went out of her way to be polite to him. He hadn't heard a single negative comment about the bread pudding escape her lips, and that puzzled him. Actually, it made him nervous. He had the impression that the Lord wanted to show him something, but Ethan wasn't quite ready to listen.

Why could she handle this better than he? If he'd been in her shoes, he'd be inclined to quit and never come back. In the event that he came back, he'd have demanded that his opinion be heard.

Dana hadn't done any of those things. She was obviously very committed to her job and loyal to the Gradys—one of the things that had attracted him to her. Didn't everyone want to fall in love with someone so intensely loyal?

When she got off the phone, she looked at him expectantly. "Hi, Ethan."

"Hi, Dana. How have you been?" He tried to ease into conversation.

She shrugged. "Busy. Very busy, but that's a good thing because it means business is going well."

"Exactly," Ethan agreed.

"Did you need something? I'm not trying to rush you, but I'm scheduled for a business lunch with Mia down in advertising."

"Oh," said Ethan. "I wanted to ask you to lunch with me."

His words seemed to surprise her because she didn't say anything for a long time. "Maybe tomorrow?" she asked. "Would that work for you?"

"Well, no," Ethan told her. "Mr. Grady and I met this morning, and we decided that today will be my last day to work here."

Dana's eyes widened. "Oh? Already?"

He nodded. "Yeah, it looks like things are going well, and I won't be needed unless there's a problem with something."

Dana opened her mouth, then closed it. She sat up straight

and clasped her hands together on the desk. He had a feeling she was trying hard to keep from mentioning the bread pudding. Again, her level of self-control amazed him.

"So what happens next for you?" she asked.

"I'm flying back to New York in the morning."

Dana nodded and gave him a tight smile. "Oh. Well, I'll be sad to see you go."

He chuckled. "You don't have to be so mournful. I'm just going to check on some things and take care of business. I'll be back in a week or so."

"Are you. . .still moving here?"

"I think so. I need to look for possible locations and things like that. It's still in the beginning stages, but I'm pretty sure the Lord wants me to stay in St. Louis."

When Dana didn't say anything, he leaned forward. "I've been praying about us. I miss you."

"I miss you too," she said without hesitation. "But where does that put us?"

Ethan sighed. Breaking up might be hard, but making up was plain old confusing. "I guess that's up to us. I still love you, and we have some things to sort out, but I don't think it's impossible."

Dana nodded slowly. "I'm willing to think about it. Why don't you call me when you get back, and we'll talk?"

"Sure." He grinned. "It'd be nice if you'd pick up the phone instead of letting the answering machine do the dirty work. I promise I'll be on my best behavior."

Dana laughed, and Ethan realized how long it had been since he'd really heard her voice, let alone a laugh. This reunion had turned out to be good for both of them.

"If I'm at home, you'll hear my voice and not the machine. I promise."

"I'll call," Ethan repeated as he got up to leave.

"Take care."

Ethan left the building feeling better than he had in weeks. He was eager to visit his parents and sister but sad to be leaving the place he had come to love as home.

His life was going well and would only get better if he could repair his relationship with Dana. For the present, he couldn't do a thing about it besides pray. This was something he'd have to address when he returned.

❧

Dana watched Ethan drive away, her mind taunting her with thoughts of what might have been. Was he really going to come back? Did he really want to continue their relationship?

At least she had managed to keep her mouth shut about the bread pudding. The more she thought about it, the sillier the whole disagreement seemed. There was no reason why two adults should get so worked up over something so trivial. If they really loved each other, they should be able to forget it and move on. She was ready to. Did Ethan feel the same?

❧

"I'm having a tea for my Sunday school class this Tuesday," Ethan's mother told him. "Do you think you could make a dessert for me?"

Ethan chuckled. He'd been home less than twenty-four hours, and already his mother wanted him to cook something. In her circle of friends, it was a well-known fact that Hannah Miles loved to entertain but hated to cook. Consequently, anytime she held an event in her home, whatever she served was usually prepared by someone else.

"Sure, Mom. What do you want me to make?"

She grinned and pinched his cheek as though he were a

baby and not a twenty-nine-year-old man. Ethan did his best to smile. Mothers.

"Make whatever you want, Sweetie. I've been having lemon bars and chicken salad lately, so they'd probably appreciate something different."

# twelve

Dana scanned the long hallway, searching for Ethan. She'd volunteered to pick him up from the airport, but to her dismay, she arrived fifteen minutes late. *He's probably wondering if I did this on purpose.* She eased past a group of travelers who had stopped moving, apparently unsure of where to go next.

"Dana!"

She turned around and caught a glimpse of Ethan, waving to get her attention. She returned the wave and began making her way back toward the other end of terminal.

The terminal at Lambert Field was especially crowded this morning, and as Dana moved through the throngs of people, she imagined herself and Ethan as characters in a movie. She was the heroine, and Ethan was the hero, finally reunited after a long separation. Once they reached each other they would fall into each other's arms, and all would be well.

Predictably, her reunion with Ethan ended up distinctly anticlimactic. There was no falling into one another's arms. Ethan shifted his luggage to his other shoulder and said, "Hi."

"Hi. Sorry I'm late. I got caught in traffic."

"That's okay," he assured her. "I just finished claiming my bags, so it worked out fine."

"So where do I need to take you?"

"My condo. The lease is about to run out, and I need to sign a new one."

This certainly seemed like encouraging news. "So you are staying?"

"Let's walk and talk," Ethan suggested.

"Can I carry something?"

"No, it's not that heavy. Which lot are you in?"

"Follow me," Dana said.

"To answer your question, I am staying. You didn't think I would come back?"

Dana smiled. "Not really. I figured once you got back to New York, you would decide you really preferred to be there."

"No way. I like too many things about this place." He gave her a meaningful look. "I'm here to stay."

They were silent for the remainder of the trek to the car, and Dana tried to think of some way to fill in the awkward gap in conversation. They were sidestepping the real issue, but she didn't want to bring it up and run the risk of sounding pushy.

"Have you had lunch yet?" Ethan asked.

"No. How about you?"

Ethan shrugged. "Plane food, but that's about it. Do you want to stop somewhere?"

"Okay. I need to get back to work in a couple of hours, but I haven't left the office for lunch all week."

"If they need you, they have your pager number," Ethan said. "On second thought, you keep everything running so well, they probably don't even notice you're gone."

Dana lifted her eyebrows. "I hope that's a compliment. It almost sounds like you're saying they don't need me."

Ethan laughed. "You know good and well that's a compliment. You really are good at your job."

Dana smiled at him. She could get used to his praise. "Okay, Ethan, you don't have to flatter me. I think we both want to pick up where we left off, so there's no need to try and butter me up."

Ethan actually looked hurt, and Dana wanted to take the words back. Maybe he'd actually just been saying those things just to be nice.

She sighed. "You know what? I'm making a mess of this. I don't know if you feel this too, but I'm just at a loss for words ever since. . .you know."

Ethan nodded. "Yeah, it's almost like we don't know how to talk to each other anymore."

Dana felt relieved. "At least I'm not the only one who feels like that."

"I'm sorry about my attitude," Ethan said. "I've been trying to justify how I acted, and the Lord isn't letting me get away with it."

Dana nodded, willing herself to be quiet so she wouldn't say something to get herself in trouble. Although she felt like asking if he still thought his bread pudding should remain in the stores, her conscience prevented her from doing so.

"So will you forgive me?"

"I've already forgiven you, Ethan. I know I've been avoiding you, but it's only because I've been working on my own struggles. I tried to hide it, but every time one of your recipes passed the survey test, it was hard for me. I guess my idea of what the customers wanted was pretty different from what they ended up liking."

"You were right about a lot of things. Remember, several of the recipes went back to the test kitchen for extra work."

Dana pulled the car into the lot of a small restaurant. "Is soup okay with you?"

"I don't really have a preference. But before we go in, I want to make sure everything is back to normal."

Dana shook her head. "No, we can't go back to normal. Because if I go back to the way I used to be, I'll still have the same problems. We have to grow and change all throughout our lives. Sometimes going back to the old way is comfortable but not necessarily the right thing to do."

Ethan nodded quietly. "I guess that's what I meant. I'm

changing too. I can't promise that I won't get on your nerves sometimes or that I'll always say or do the right thing. But I have been working on some things lately. I don't want to ruin this relationship again."

Dana was pleased to hear him say that. Looking back, she could see they both had come a long way.

"Tell me, Dana, are you willing to continue this relationship? I still love you."

She bit her lip, hesitating. On the one hand, she was happy Ethan still loved her, but she didn't feel entirely comfortable picking up where they had left off. They almost needed to be reacquainted.

Ethan picked up on her silence and reached out for her hand. "Dana, you have to tell me what's wrong. Is it the list? Am I not close enough to your ideal?"

Dana blinked. How did he know about that? "What?" she asked him.

Ethan looked chagrined, and she realized he hadn't meant to let her know that he knew.

"How do you know about the list?" she questioned again.

"Well. . .I wasn't supposed to tell you."

"You're not even supposed to know I had written one. The least you can do is tell me how you heard about it."

"Your brothers. We were talking one day, they mentioned it, and I got them to tell me the whole story. I worried that you weren't very serious about me, and they made some jokes about your ideal."

"Oh." Dana paused, thinking. She didn't even have to ask to know that Albert and Anthony were in on this. They would be the main culprits. She wondered exactly what they had said.

"So exactly what did they tell you?"

"Do I have to answer that?"

"Yes," she said. When he didn't reply immediately, she poked him in the arm with her finger. "I'm waiting." Ethan looked so embarrassed, she felt like laughing.

"They didn't really go into specifics, but they told me that your notions were pretty confusing. They told me you wanted to marry somebody like Mr. Darcy from *Pride and Prejudice.*"

"They what?" Her brothers certainly had managed to confuse things. "I never said that. I never even wrote that. I have no idea where they got such a crazy idea."

Ethan shrugged. "Maybe they didn't understand the list."

Obviously, they hadn't. "You can say that again. I liked some qualities in Mr. Darcy, but I would never be happy to end up with someone exactly like him. At least, not the way he acted early in the book. I wanted a husband who could be sweet and kind, but I need him to be strong and a good leader. He would be. . ." Dana trailed off. Ethan was hanging onto her every word, and she didn't want to contribute to this mess any further. "Never mind. The fact is, I outgrew the list. It doesn't make any difference anymore."

Ethan grinned. "You're sure about that?"

"Positive," Dana said emphatically. "It's not about a list; it's about who God knows I'll be happy with. If I met a guy who had every quality I ever dreamed of, I'd still have to make sure God wanted us to be together. If He said no, my plans would not have done me a bit of good."

"So if Mr. Darcy came knocking on your door one morning, you'd turn him away."

Dana grinned. "Well, let's not be so hasty. I'd at least let him come in and have some tea."

Ethan laughed. "Aha! What happened to the prayer?"

"I'd pray while I made the tea," Dana said in her defense. "I couldn't just let Mr. Darcy, himself, get away."

"Yeah, I'll bet. Somehow, that doesn't surprise me."

"Laugh all you want." Dana opened the car door. "But I'm going in to get some soup. You can either sit out here and make jokes about Mr. Darcy, or you can come in and have lunch with me."

Ethan followed. "I'll come inside. We can always talk about Mr. Darcy later." He continued laughing as they entered the restaurant.

Dana shook her head. Her brothers were going to have some serious explaining to do for divulging her silly high school secrets like that.

&

The next day, Mr. Grady stopped in Dana's office early one morning and said, "It's time to do the award for Manager of the Year. The annual employee appreciation dinner is in two weeks."

"Wow, time has really flown by this year," said Dana "Who's the lucky manager?"

"Kim Penn. She has an excellent work ethic, and her employees are so productive. She really knows how to get the best out of people." He shrugged. "She's a lot like you."

Dana smiled. She was so thankful that Mr. Grady had forgiven her for her outburst. He had apologized for overreacting but stood firm in his decision to support Ethan's bread pudding until it could be determined whether or not it would eventually be productive in terms of sales.

"What do you think? Will Kim be excited?"

Dana grinned. "She'll be thrilled." Kim had spent the entire year going after this award. Of course, it wasn't exactly a major distinction in terms of the outside world, but within the Grady Company, the achievement was greatly respected.

"So you'll see to it that the certificate is drawn up?"

"Of course," said Dana.

"I also have more news," he said, taking a seat. "I got a call from Ethan this morning. He got back in town yesterday."

Dana nodded. "Yes, we had lunch together."

Mr. Grady smiled approvingly. "We had a long talk, and I thought you'd be interested in knowing that he's asked me to remove the pumpernickel bread pudding from the menu."

Dana was shocked. "He what?"

Mr. Grady shook his head. "He's asked me to remove it from the menu. He says he hasn't worked with it enough and doesn't think it's a good fit for our stores."

Dana tried to find her voice. She had to be careful not to gloat. "Well, Sir, if that's the way he feels. . ."

Mr. Grady laughed. "Dana, you don't have to pretend with me. I've been hearing from customers, managers, and my wife about the dish. I've been watching the sales records, and to tell you the truth, I'm relieved he called me. You were right; it was an unwise use of time, money, and display space. I planned to call him next week and tell him we needed to pull it."

Mr. Grady stood up. "You've got a good head on your shoulders, and I'm proud to have you working for us. Thanks so much for sticking it out with us, even when you were unhappy with me."

He shook his head. "I guess we all make our mistakes, and I just got so thrilled to be mentioned in *Restaurant Owner* that I took leave of my senses for awhile. Thanks for cutting me and Ethan some slack."

Tears came to Dana's eyes. "Thank you, Mr. Grady. It's really been a honor to work for you, and I look forward to many more years of the same."

Mr. Grady shook his head and waved her comment away. "Nonsense. I know pretty soon Ethan will want you working at his restaurant—especially since you two plan to get married. We'll be sorry to see you go, but we'll send you off with our best wishes." He turned and left the room before she could even answer him.

Dana sat at her desk, thinking about several things. First, she was thankful Ethan had been brave enough to pull his recipe. She still felt curious about what had prompted the decision, but there was no way she would pry into his business.

The second thing that puzzled her was Mr. Grady's remark about her getting married. While they had talked about marriage since Ethan's return, he still had yet to propose to her.

Could he be planning something? Dana smiled, wondering how he would try to surprise her.

Before she could get too wrapped up in her own thoughts, Dana remembered her promise to Mr. Grady to take care of Kim's award. She needed to have a certificate done, along with a plaque with Kim's name engraved on it.

She made a call to Betty, who was in charge of all employee records and asked to have something with Kim's name on it sent to her office. The last thing she wanted to do was have Kim's name misspelled on the award.

Twenty minutes later, Betty delivered a piece of paper with Kim's name on it. At least, it was supposed to be Kim's name. According to this paper, Kim's full name was Kimetra F. Penn.

Dana stared at the sheet. Kimetra? And what did the "F" stand for? Remembering that Kim wasn't particularly fond of her middle name put Dana in a dilemma. Would Kim want the plaque to read Kim or Kimetra? Would she want the middle initial totally omitted, or would she prefer it remain there since it was a special award?

The more Dana thought about it, the more confusing it became.

Finally, she decided to give Kim a call. She might have to give away the surprise about the award, but she would rather let the cat out of the bag than put the wrong name on the plaque. She dialed the number to Kim's office. Kim picked up on the third ring.

"Hi, it's Dana," she said.

"Hi, Dana. I'm surprised you caught me at my desk. You wouldn't believe the crowd we've had this morning."

"Excellent," said Dana. "That's good news."

"No kidding," Kim agreed. "There was a time I thought I'd go nuts if I heard another customer complain that his sandwich was all wrong, but I'll tell you, after some of the slow days we had during our slump, customer noise is music to my ears."

Dana laughed. "I won't keep you long, but it's come to my attention that your full name is Kimetra F. Penn."

Kim didn't say a word.

"Hello? Kim, are you still there?"

"Dana, who told you that?"

"Actually, I had Betty look up your file—"

Kim inhaled sharply, then interrupted her. "Dana, I can't believe you went snooping in the files to see if you could find my middle name. I'm actually pretty offended right now."

"Kim, please hear me out. I would never do that, and I can't go into details because you're not supposed to know this yet, but I needed to know the correct spelling of your name for something concerning work."

"What?"

"When I saw your name here in the file, I realized you probably didn't want your entire name on this work related thing, so I called you to check on your preference."

Kim didn't speak for several moments, then she let out a squeal. "Oh, you're kidding! I'm Manager of the Year? Is that it?"

"I'm not allowed to tell you that, but I do need to know your name preference. And I'm pretty curious as to what that 'F' stands for."

Kim squealed again. "You know what Dana? You have made my day. And if you have them put plain old K-i-m P-e-n-n on my plaque, I will be eternally grateful."

Dana decided to tease her friend a bit. "Exactly how grateful?"

Kim groaned. "I'll tell you my middle name if you promise never to reveal it."

Dana smiled. "Really? I was just kidding, you know."

"I know I don't have to tell you, but I'm in a pretty good mood. First, I will warn you that I have no idea what my parents were thinking."

Dana shrugged. "It can't be that bad."

"Yes, it can. They wanted to pick something that flowed into my last name, so they figured the perfect choice of a middle name was. . ."

Silence sounded from the other end. "Come on, Kim, you can't change your mind now. I'm hanging on your every word."

"Hold your horses, Dana. I was checking outside the door to make sure no one is listening."

"Oh. So what is it?"

"Fountain."

"Fountain? That's not so bad."

"Could you a be a little quieter, Dana? You don't have to go tell it on the mountain."

"I'm not talking that loud," Dana protested. Suddenly, the effect of Kim's full name sunk in. "Fountain Penn?" Dana felt an attack of the giggles coming on, but for Kim's sake, she held them back.

"Yeah," Kim grumbled. "Kimetra Fountain Penn. They thought it sounded graceful."

"Wow," was all Dana could say without bursting into laughter.

"Listen, Dana, I've got a crowd out front. Don't ever

mention this again, and please make sure there is no hint of my full name on the plaque. Got it?"

"Got it," Dana agreed. "And don't worry; my lips are sealed."

"They'd better be," Kim warned playfully. "And I'm sorry for overreacting earlier. I should have realized you wouldn't try to embarrass me on purpose. I'll talk to you later."

As soon as Dana hung up the phone, the giggles escaped. She couldn't believe Kim's middle name was actually Fountain. Talk about parents with a sense of humor!

Still, she felt glad her own parents hadn't opted to give her such an unusual middle name. Plain old Marie worked fine for her.

As she wrote Kim's name preference on a sheet of paper to send to the engravers, she started laughing all over again.

"Did I miss a joke?"

Dana would know that voice anywhere. She glanced up to find Ethan standing in her doorway.

"Hey, what brings you here this morning?"

He shrugged. "I had something I needed to do." Taking a step closer, he asked, "So what is so funny?"

Dana shook her head. "Just something Kim told me. Mr. Grady came in a little earlier." He nodded, and Dana chose her next words very carefully. "That was really understanding of you to pull the bread pudding. I know how much it meant to you."

Ethan sat in the chair in front of her desk. "You don't have to pretend I'm that gallant. The truth is, I convinced myself you hated that recipe because you don't like pumpernickel. When I went home, I made it for my mom's Sunday school tea. That's when I realized it wasn't working.

"Nobody wanted to be rude, so after everyone tasted it, my mom said they all suddenly remembered they were allergic to one of the ingredients. And my mom, who likes everything I make, confessed she had to force herself to swallow the one bite she tasted.

"She sent me to the store to buy some shortbread cookies, and by the time I got back, all traces of that dish had disappeared. My mom threw the entire thing out." Ethan shook his head. "She said she couldn't pin down any one flavor, and it seemed too complicated."

Dana smiled. "I'm glad she was honest with you."

"So am I," Ethan agreed. "I guess I had been a little egotistical because no one has ever flat out said that something I made tasted horrible." Shrugging, he added, "I guess there's a first time for everything."

"We all mess up sometimes," Dana said, trying to console him. He still seemed a little miffed, and she didn't want to rub his nose in it.

"I told my mom what had happened with us, and she gave me a piece of her mind. She sent me back with her own apologies that you had to put up with me."

Dana nodded. She could remember days in the not-so-distant past when she couldn't wait for Ethan to see the extent of his wrongs. Now that he had and was genuinely sorry, it hurt to see how badly he felt.

"Ethan, really, it's all been forgiven. I mean that. So how about putting this chapter behind us? I mean, we can't say we'll never make mistakes again, but at least we won't repeat this whole fiasco."

"I like the sound of that," said Ethan.

"We've both had our problems with pride, but we're working on getting our noses out of the air."

"Right. And we'll put the pumpernickel behind us too," said Ethan.

"You don't know how much I appreciate that." Dana laughed. "Who would have ever guessed bread pudding would cause such a ruckus?"

"Now that we've left pride and pumpernickel in the past, I want to talk about our future," said Ethan.

He got out of his chair and came around to her side of the desk. He stood awkwardly next to her for several moments, then dropped down to one knee.

Dana instantly knew what he would say, and this time she was ready. Ethan wasn't the perfect man, but she wasn't the perfect woman. With God's grace, they would be able to see past their differences.

*Thank you Lord, for sending Ethan to me. Who needs Mr. Darcy, anyway?*

Ethan reached for her hand and cleared his throat. "Okay, I'm going to warn you beforehand that I won't be able to do this as well as Mr. Darcy, but I will get straight to the point.

"I love you, Dana Marie Edwards. And I know I've caused some problems by being stubborn, but like you said, we've put all that behind us. That said. . ." He paused and reached into his pocket and pulled out a small jewelry box. "I'd be honored if we can move forward with our lives together. Would you marry me?"

Tears came to Dana's eyes, even as she thought of all the times she had promised herself she would not cry when her future husband proposed to her. She fanned her eyes with her free hand trying to stop the tears before they started rolling down her cheeks.

"I will," she said and hugged Ethan.

In the midst of her tears, she noticed the sheet of paper with Kim's name on it. Kim's advice about marriage trivia popped into her head, and Dana chuckled. Pulling away from Ethan, she cleared her throat. Trying to sound serious, she said, "Wait a minute. Before I can commit to this, I need to know something."

Ethan looked puzzled. "You're changing your mind?"

"It depends. . . ." she said mysteriously.

"On what?" The look on his face was priceless, a mixture of panic and confusion.

Doing her best to keep a straight face, she said, "I have to know your middle name."

Ethan shook his head. "You don't want to know my middle name."

Dana couldn't believe he was actually trying to get out of the question. It was so simple, and after all, he knew her middle name. "Yes, I do, Mr. Ethan D. Miles."

He sighed. "Fine. Did I ever tell you how much my mother liked *Pride and Prejudice?*"

Dana nodded. "I remember you saying that once or twice."

"Well she really. . .really liked it."

"You're changing the subject. Now tell me your middle name. I demand to know."

Ethan leaned closer to her until his face was inches away from hers. He leaned forward a bit more, and Dana knew he would kiss her.

She moved away, shaking her head. "No. No middle name, no kiss," she laughed.

Ethan groaned. "I can't believe you're making me tell you." He put his arms around her again. "Ethan Darcy Miles."

Dana blinked. "Did you say. . .Darcy?"

Ethan nodded. "It's a horrible name for any little boy, especially when you're in the third grade and some of the older kids start teasing you about it. We will never give that name to any of our children."

Dana giggled, but Ethan shook his head. "Furthermore, I have guarded this name for years, and no one outside of my immediate family knows what the D. in my name stands for."

"I won't tell," Dana grumbled. This was too good to be true.

She was in the arms of her own living, breathing Mr. Darcy.

Ethan shook his head. "That's not good enough. Since you know my secret, you have no choice but to marry me now."

As he leaned in to kiss her, Dana answered, "Gladly. . .Mr. Darcy."

# A Letter To Our Readers

Dear Reader:

In order that we might better contribute to your reading enjoyment, we would appreciate your taking a few minutes to respond to the following questions. We welcome your comments and read each form and letter we receive. When completed, please return to the following:

Rebecca Germany, Fiction Editor
Heartsong Presents
PO Box 719
Uhrichsville, Ohio 44683

1. Did you enjoy reading *Pride and Pumpernickel* by Aisha Ford?

   ❏ Very much! I would like to see more books
      by this author!
   ❏ Moderately. I would have enjoyed it more if

   _____

   _____

2. Are you a member of **Heartsong Presents**?  Yes ❏  No ❏
   If no, where did you purchase this book?_____

   _____

3. How would you rate, on a scale from 1 (poor) to 5 (superior), the cover design?_____

4. On a scale from 1 (poor) to 10 (superior), please rate the following elements.

   _____ Heroine      _____ Plot

   _____ Hero         _____ Inspirational theme

   _____ Setting      _____ Secondary characters

5. These characters were special because _____

_____

_____

6. How has this book inspired your life? _____

_____

_____

7. What settings would you like to see covered in future **Heartsong Presents** books? _____

_____

_____

8. What are some inspirational themes you would like to see treated in future books? _____

_____

_____

9. Would you be interested in reading other **Heartsong Presents** titles?         Yes ☐            No ☐

10. Please check your age range:
     ☐ Under 18          ☐ 18-24          ☐ 25-34
     ☐ 35-45             ☐ 46-55          ☐ Over 55

Name _____

Occupation _____

Address _____

City _____ State _____ Zip _____

Email _____

# City DREAMS

$\mathscr{L}$eaving their rural Nebraska home far behind, the Delacourt sisters—Sharon, Danielle, Sabrina, and Denise—have chosen to pursue their dreams in a big city. Set on making an impact on the world, will they meet disappointment or delight?

Life in the city offers new challenges, new lessons, and new loves. Will these four young women see their new world through God's eyes and rise to their opportunities like the surrounding skyscrapers?

paperback, 352 pages, 5 ³⁄₁₆" x 8"

❤ ❤ ❤ ❤ ❤ ❤ ❤ ❤ ❤ ❤ ❤ ❤ ❤ ❤ ❤ ❤ ❤ ❤ ❤ ❤

Please send me _____ copies of *City Dreams*. I am enclosing $5.97 for each. (Please add $2.00 to cover postage and handling per order. OH add 6% tax.)

Send check or money order, no cash or C.O.D.s please.

Name_____

Address _____

City, State, Zip _____

**To place a credit card order, call 1-800-847-8270.**
Send to: Heartsong Presents Reader Service, PO Box 721, Uhrichsville, OH 44683
❤ ❤ ❤ ❤ ❤ ❤ ❤ ❤ ❤ ❤ ❤ ❤ ❤ ❤ ❤ ❤ ❤ ❤ ❤ ❤

# Heart♥ong

## CONTEMPORARY ROMANCE IS CHEAPER BY THE DOZEN!

**Buy any assortment of twelve *Heartsong Presents* titles and save 25% off of the already discounted price of $2.95 each!**

*Any 12 Heartsong Presents titles for only $27.00\**

*\*plus $2.00 shipping and handling per order and sales tax where applicable.*

## HEARTSONG PRESENTS *TITLES AVAILABLE NOW:*

\_\_HP177 NEPALI NOON, *S. Hayden*
\_\_HP178 EAGLES FOR ANNA, *C. Runyon*
\_\_HP181 RETREAT TO LOVE, *N. Rue*
\_\_HP182 A WING AND A PRAYER, *T. Peterson*
\_\_HP186 WINGS LIKE EAGLES, *T. Peterson*
\_\_HP189 A KINDLED SPARK, *C. Reece*
\_\_HP193 COMPASSIONATE LOVE, *A. Bell*
\_\_HP194 WAIT FOR THE MORNING, *K. Baez*
\_\_HP197 EAGLE PILOT, *J. Stengl*
\_\_HP201 A WHOLE NEW WORLD, *Y. Lehman*
\_\_HP205 A QUESTION OF BALANCE, *V. B. Jones*
\_\_HP206 POLITICALLY CORRECT, *K. Cornelius*
\_\_HP209 SOFT BEATS MY HEART, *A. Carter*
\_\_HP210 THE FRUIT OF HER HANDS, *J. Orcutt*
\_\_HP213 PICTURE OF LOVE, *T. H. Murray*
\_\_HP214 TOMORROW'S RAINBOW, *V. Wiggins*
\_\_HP217 ODYSSEY OF LOVE, *M. Panagiotopoulos*
\_\_HP218 HAWAIIAN HEARTBEAT, *Y.Lehman*
\_\_HP221 THIEF OF MY HEART, *C. Bach*
\_\_HP222 FINALLY, LOVE, *J. Stengl*
\_\_HP225 A ROSE IS A ROSE, *R. R. Jones*
\_\_HP226 WINGS OF THE DAWN, *T. Peterson*
\_\_HP233 FAITH CAME LATE, *F. Chrisman*
\_\_HP234 GLOWING EMBERS, *C. L. Reece*
\_\_HP237 THE NEIGHBOR, *D. W. Smith*
\_\_HP238 ANNIE'S SONG, *A. Boeshaar*
\_\_HP242 FAR ABOVE RUBIES, *B. Melby and C. Wienke*

\_\_HP245 CROSSROADS, *T. Peterson and J. Peterson*
\_\_HP246 BRIANNA'S PARDON, *G. Clover*
\_\_HP254 THE REFUGE, *R. Simons*
\_\_HP261 RACE OF LOVE, *M. Panagiotopoulos*
\_\_HP262 HEAVEN'S CHILD, *G. Fields*
\_\_HP265 HEARTH OF FIRE, *C. L. Reece*
\_\_HP266 WHAT LOVE REMEMBERS, *M. G. Chapman*
\_\_HP269 WALKING THE DOG, *G. Sattler*
\_\_HP270 PROMISE ME FOREVER, *A. Boeshaar*
\_\_HP273 SUMMER PLACE, *P. Darty*
\_\_HP274 THE HEALING PROMISE, *H. Alexander*
\_\_HP277 ONCE MORE WITH FEELING, *B. Bancroft*
\_\_HP278 ELIZABETH'S CHOICE, *L. Lyle*
\_\_HP282 THE WEDDING WISH, *L. Lough*
\_\_HP289 THE PERFECT WIFE, *G. Fields*
\_\_HP297 A THOUSAND HILLS, *R. McCollum*
\_\_HP298 A SENSE OF BELONGING, *T. Fowler*
\_\_HP302 SEASONS, *G. G. Martin*
\_\_HP305 CALL OF THE MOUNTAIN, *Y. Lehman*
\_\_HP306 PIANO LESSONS, *G. Sattler*
\_\_HP310 THE RELUCTANT BRIDE, *H. Spears*
\_\_HP317 LOVE REMEMBERED, *A. Bell*
\_\_HP318 BORN FOR THIS LOVE, *B. Bancroft*
\_\_HP321 FORTRESS OF LOVE, *M. Panagiotopoulos*
\_\_HP322 COUNTRY CHARM, *D. Mills*
\_\_HP325 GONE CAMPING, *G. Sattler*
\_\_HP326 A TENDER MELODY, *B. L. Etchison*
\_\_HP329 MEET MY SISTER, TESS, *K. Billerbeck*
\_\_HP330 DREAMING OF CASTLES, *G. G. Martin*
\_\_HP337 OZARK SUNRISE, *H. Alexander*
\_\_HP338 SOMEWHERE A RAINBOW, *Y. Lehman*
\_\_HP341 IT ONLY TAKES A SPARK, *P. K. Tracy*
\_\_HP342 THE HAVEN OF REST, *A. Boeshaar*
\_\_HP346 DOUBLE TAKE, *T. Fowler*

(If ordering from this page, please remember to include it with the order form.)

# ·······Presents·······

| | |
|---|---|
| _HP349 WILD TIGER WIND, *G. Buck* | _HP418 YESTERYEAR, *G. Brandt* |
| _HP350 RACE FOR THE ROSES, *L. Snelling* | _HP421 LOOKING FOR A MIRACLE, |
| _HP353 ICE CASTLE, *J. Livingston* | *W. E. Brunstetter* |
| _HP354 FINDING COURTNEY, *B. L. Etchison* | _HP422 CONDO MANIA, *M. G. Chapman* |
| _HP357 WHITER THAN SNOW, *Y. Lehman* | _HP425 MUSTERING COURAGE, *L. A. Coleman* |
| _HP358 AT ARM'S LENGTH, *G. Sattler* | _HP426 TO THE EXTREME, *T. Davis* |
| _HP361 THE NAME GAME, *M. G. Chapman* | _HP429 LOVE AHOY, *C. Coble* |
| _HP362 STACY'S WEDDING, *A. Ford* | _HP430 GOOD THINGS COME, *J. A. Ryan* |
| _HP365 STILL WATERS, *G. Fields* | _HP433 A FEW FLOWERS, *G. Sattler* |
| _HP366 TO GALILEE WITH LOVE, *E. M. Berger* | _HP434 FAMILY CIRCLE, *J. L. Barton* |
| _HP370 TWIN VICTORIES, *C. M. Hake* | _HP437 NORTHERN EXPOSURE, *J. Livingston* |
| _HP373 CATCH OF A LIFETIME, *Y. Lehman* | _HP438 OUT IN THE REAL WORLD, *K. Paul* |
| _HP377 COME HOME TO MY HEART, | _HP441 CASSIDY'S CHARM, *D. Mills* |
| *J. A. Grote* | _HP442 VISION OF HOPE, *M. H. Flinkman* |
| _HP378 THE LANDLORD TAKES A BRIDE, | _HP445 MCMILLIAN'S MATCHMAKERS, |
| *K. Billerbeck* | *G. Sattler* |
| _HP381 SOUTHERN SYMPATHIES, *A. Boeshaar* | _HP446 ANGELS TO WATCH OVER ME, |
| _HP382 THE BRIDE WORE BOOTS, *J. Livingston* | *P. Griffin* |
| _HP390 LOVE ABOUNDS, *A. Bell* | _HP449 AN OSTRICH A DAY, *N. J. Farrier* |
| _HP394 EQUESTRIAN CHARM, *D. Mills* | _HP450 LOVE IN PURSUIT, *D. Mills* |
| _HP401 CASTLE IN THE CLOUDS, *A. Boeshaar* | _HP453 THE ELUSIVE MR. PERFECT, |
| _HP402 SECRET BALLOT, *Y. Lehman* | *T. H. Murray* |
| _HP405 THE WIFE DEGREE, *A. Ford* | _HP454 GRACE IN ACTION, *K. Billerbeck* |
| _HP406 ALMOST TWINS, *G. Sattler* | _HP457 A ROSE AMONG THORNS, *L. Bliss* |
| _HP409 A LIVING SOUL, *H. Alexander* | _HP458 THE CANDY CANE CALABOOSE, |
| _HP410 THE COLOR OF LOVE, *D. Mills* | *J. Spaeth* |
| _HP413 REMNANT OF VICTORY, *J. Odell* | _HP461 PRIDE AND PUMPERNICKEL, *A. Ford* |
| _HP414 THE SEA BECKONS, *B. L. Etchison* | _HP462 SECRETS WITHIN, *G. G. Martin* |
| _HP417 FROM RUSSIA WITH LOVE, *C. Coble* | |

## Great Inspirational Romance at a Great Price!

**Heartsong Presents** books are inspirational romances in contemporary and historical settings, designed to give you an enjoyable, spirit-lifting reading experience. You can choose wonderfully written titles from some of today's best authors like Hannah Alexander, Irene B. Brand, Yvonne Lehman, Tracie Peterson, and many others.

*When ordering quantities less than twelve, above titles are $2.95 each.*

*Not all titles may be available at time of order.*

---

SEND TO: **Heartsong Presents** Reader's Service
P.O. Box 721, Uhrichsville, Ohio 44683

Please send me the items checked above. I am enclosing $_____
(please add $2.00 to cover postage per order. OH add 6.25% tax. NJ add 6%.). Send check or money order, no cash or C.O.D.s, please.
**To place a credit card order, call 1-800-847-8270.**

NAME _____

ADDRESS _____

CITY/STATE _____ ZIP _____

HPS 13-01

# Hearts♥ng Presents
## *Love Stories Are Rated G!*

That's for godly, gratifying, and of course, great! If you love a thrilling love story but don't appreciate the sordidness of some popular paperback romances, **Heartsong Presents** is for you. In fact, **Heartsong Presents** is the *only inspirational romance book club* featuring love stories where Christian faith is the primary ingredient in a marriage relationship.

Sign up today to receive your first set of four never-before-published Christian romances. Send no money now; you will receive a bill with the first shipment. You may cancel at any time without obligation, and if you aren't completely satisfied with any selection, you may return the books for an immediate refund!

Imagine. . .four new romances every four weeks—two historical, two contemporary—with men and women like you who long to meet the one God has chosen as the love of their lives. . .all for the low price of $9.97 postpaid.

*To join, simply complete the coupon below and mail to the address provided.* **Heartsong Presents** romances are rated G for another reason: They'll arrive *Godspeed!*

---

# YES! Sign me up for Heartsong!

**NEW MEMBERSHIPS WILL BE SHIPPED IMMEDIATELY!**
**Send no money now.** We'll bill you only $9.97 post-paid with your first shipment of four books. Or for faster action, call toll free 1-800-847-8270.

NAME _____

ADDRESS _____

CITY _____ STATE _____ ZIP _____

MAIL TO: HEARTSONG PRESENTS, PO Box 721, Uhrichsville, Ohio 44683

YES10-96